GHOST IN THE HEADLIGHTS

GHOST IN THE HEADLIGHTS

LINDSEY DUGA

Scholastic Inc.

ISBN 978-1-338-63095-4

10 9 8 7 6 5 4 3   21 22 23 24 25

Printed in the U.S.A.   40
First printing 2021

Book design by Stephanie Yang

To Dad

1

The black clouds swallowed up the moon. It hadn't been this dark when she'd started out for the evening. In fact, the setting sun had been such a bright, beautiful orange that it looked a bit like her prizewinning pumpkin, which now felt heavy in her arms. But she didn't dare put it down in case it got dirty.

Her father would be so proud of her. A pumpkin she'd grown herself. And it had won first place, too. She hummed her favorite little tune to make the walk home go faster.

The farmer in the dell...

The farmer in the dell...

Hi-ho, the derry-o,

1

The farmer in the dell.

The branches rattled overhead, knocking together in the strong October wind. Leaves rolled across the asphalt, while the cries of a crow echoed down the long road. Worried about her pumpkin getting cold, she took off her sweater and wrapped the pumpkin in the light blue knit sweater her grandmother had made for her. It matched the blue ribbon tied around the stem.

With every step, the pumpkin seemed to get heavier. If she had waited for her mother, they could have walked home from the fair together, but she had wanted to show off her first-place ribbon to her father so badly. Her father had left the fair early to go home and make sure the cows were all back in the barn. Why hadn't she been just a bit more patient?

When the bend in the road finally came into view, she started to walk a little faster. Home was just around the corner.

SCREEEECH.

The sound chilled her down to her very bones. Tires screeching on concrete, a loud engine revving to demonic life. She turned to find a pair of glowing yellow orbs. They were so bright and horrifying that they felt more like the eyes of a monster than the headlights of a car. Too late did she notice that they were headed right for her, coming at her faster than the wind itself.

The monster could not be stopped. VROOOM. The roar shook the trees.

She dropped her pumpkin. Heart in her throat, she tried to get off the road—run for the trees. Her feet pounded across the pavement—fast but not fast enough. Over the sound of her footsteps, she could hear the angry engine, she could feel the heat of the headlights, smell the gasoline, taste the burning rubber of tires—

∽ 🎃 ∾

"Ouch!"

Brianna awoke with a start, her feet kicking out reflexively and hitting something solid.

Shaking off the remnants of the terrifying dream, Brianna brushed her brown hair away from her cheeks. The flight attendant who'd been sitting with her for the last half hour scowled at Brianna and rubbed her shin. Clearly it had been *her* shin that Brianna had accidentally kicked.

"Sorry!" Brianna said hurriedly, sitting up in her

chair and wiping away any drool that had come from her impromptu nap. A nap that had been interrupted by a strange yet very realistic dream. Even though she'd never won a pumpkin contest in her life, or walked down a lone road holding one, it had felt more like a memory than a dream. Lately, many of her dreams had felt that way.

The backpack that Brianna had been using as a pillow fell to the ground, and the flight attendant snatched it up, handing it back to her.

"I was just about to wake you up," the flight attendant said in a snippy tone. "Your uncle is finally here."

Brianna was about to ask, *What uncle?* But then she remembered where she was and why she had fallen asleep in the Philadelphia airport.

Brianna Jenson was to stay with her estranged uncle for two whole months while her mother trained for a new job. Even now, with her suitcase packed and her uncle here to collect her from the airport, Brianna still had a hard time believing that it was actually really happening.

It had all started when her mother, a talented engineer, had been laid off at a failing plant in their hometown of Richland, Texas. She'd looked for a new job for almost half a year before stumbling upon an opportunity to work in management at a new energy plant.

Mrs. Jenson had broken the news of the opportunity to her daughter over a bacon-onion-and-pepperoni pizza from their favorite pizza place, Gino's.

"I'll be working as a manager at the plant, Bree," her mother had said around a mouthful of pizza. "Building up wind farms. You know, those rows of windmills?"

"But that's not what you do," Brianna pointed out. Truthfully, she knew very little about what her mom did, but she knew her mom didn't work with something as cool as wind.

"You're right," her mom agreed. "Which is why I have to train for it. The program lasts about two months."

"That's not so bad," Brianna said, picking up another slice.

"Well, no, but..." her mom continued hesitantly.

"Unfortunately, the management training program is in Nevada. And I can't take you with me, honey. It'll be long hours, and the training facility is too far for a school bus to come get you. And you still need to go to school."

Brianna tried to wrap her head around what her mother was saying: *Mom's going to be gone for two whole months.*

But that wasn't the worst of it. Instead of being able to stay with her friends in Richland—two months was far too long to impose on her friends' families—Brianna had no choice but to stay with her uncle, Shane, in a tiny town called Drury Gables, Pennsylvania. Uncle Shane, her mother had reminded her, was Brianna's uncle on her dad's side. Brianna couldn't remember much, but they had lived near Uncle Shane when Brianna was very young, before her dad had died and before they had moved from Drury Gables to Texas for a new start.

For days following the revelation of the "master plan," as her mother had started calling it, Brianna thought of how to get out of it: She didn't remember

Drury Gables or her life there at all, so how could she be sure she'd like it now? Even if he was family, Uncle Shane was a stranger to her, and how could she live with a stranger?

But when Brianna saw how excited her mother had become about her training program and the promise of providing a better life for the two of them, Brianna chose to keep her mouth shut. Being miserable for two months was a small price to pay for her mother's happiness and the chance to stay in Richland forever.

So, here she was, at the Philadelphia airport, rolling her suitcase packed with two months' worth of clothes, lugging her backpack with two months' worth of comic books, going to live with a stranger in a town she'd left when she was no more than three years old.

Just two months, Brianna repeated in her mind. It was starting to sound like her mantra.

Finally they reached baggage claim, where they met an older man by the door to the short-term parking area. While Uncle Shane proved who he said he was to the flight attendant, Brianna stood off to the side, inspecting him. He was medium height, taller than her mom but shorter than her gym teacher. He had a short brown beard and short brown hair, and wore old oil-stained jeans, work boots, and a flannel shirt.

Uncle Shane caught her staring, and he peered down at her with a frown, rubbing his bristly beard. "Is that all?" he asked.

Brianna blinked. "What?"

Uncle Shane gestured to the suitcase at her side. "Is that all your luggage, kid?"

"Oh!" Brianna glanced down at her bag. "Um, yeah."

"Truck's this way," he grunted as he grabbed her suitcase and carried it through the sliding doors into the parking garage. Brianna hurried to catch up, missing her chance to tell him that the suitcase could roll.

The drive to Drury Gables was beautiful, Brianna had to admit, even if the ride itself wasn't all that pleasant. She sat on the passenger side of the truck, her backpack tucked at her feet and her suitcase wedged between her and her uncle. Cluttered around the cab of the truck were various napkins and fast-food wrappers and empty Coke cans. The truck was smelly, and Brianna was tempted to roll down a window to get a breath of air that wasn't tainted by old french fries. But she didn't.

Uncle Shane had barely said a word to her since complaining about the long drive to the airport. Apparently there was a Philadelphia Eagles game that he couldn't miss.

If you didn't want to miss your game, then why'd you wait so long to pick me up? Brianna wondered as she watched the rolling hills pass by through the grimy window.

She was surprised at the difference in scenery every few miles. In their part of Texas, the land was mostly flat—pretty boring, actually. But every mile in Pennsylvania was a surprise. They passed sections of forest that opened up to bare hills, then a winding river or lake in the distance. The grass was mostly green, but Brianna could see the hint of fall in patches of gold and light brown. It was early September, and the trees still had the bulk of their emerald leaves, though some of them had begun to change.

That was one thing her mother had gotten her excited about—the autumn colors. Brianna hoped to take out her Prismacolor pencils and sketch a beautiful fall scene that she could then show to her art club teacher back home, Mrs. Brinks.

The car ride was a little less than an hour, and Brianna guessed that they were getting close when they passed an old sign with the words DRURY GABLES carved into wood, along with some pumpkins painted in orange but now peeling with age.

They went down a few streets with old brick buildings and streetlights. A church, a library, a courthouse, a grocery store, an auto repair shop, an old diner... Everything a small town needed to survive. Uncle Shane turned off the main road downtown and drove past large cornfields, the setting sun turning the stalks from a dusty yellow to hues of copper and gold. His next turn was onto a road covered in trees, and the cab of the truck suddenly grew dark from the shadows of overhanging leaves and branches. They seemed to interlock, creating a tunnel. Brianna noticed a dilapidated sign that read SHADOWRUN ROAD.

A sudden shiver overcame Brianna as she watched the patterns of shadows and sunlight flicker across the asphalt. This road was familiar somehow. Maybe it was something about the long tree line, or the way the branches crisscrossed overhead, or—

That's when Brianna remembered her dream. It seemed impossible, but she was almost positive that this road was the same road she had dreamed of, even if it was lighter outside and certainly less creepy. Brianna leaned away from the window, sucking in a breath.

"What's the matter, kid?" Uncle Shane asked, glancing down at her, then quickly directing his gaze back to the road.

"I . . . I . . ."

"Well?" Uncle Shane insisted. "Spit it out!"

"I had a dream about this road." Brianna couldn't

stop her voice from shaking. When she thought about the road, she remembered the monster that came barreling down it.

But Uncle Shane didn't seem impressed by Brianna's dream. Instead, he huffed and shrugged. "You used to go down this road with your parents a lot as a kid."

Brianna gaped at her uncle. "But I don't remember it at all!"

Uncle Shane tapped the top of her head with one strong finger. "Maybe *you* don't, but that don't mean *your mind* doesn't. Brains are weird, kid."

Brianna bit her bottom lip in an effort to prevent an argument. Maybe the dream had been a memory after all, but she was quite sure it wasn't *hers*.

Suddenly, Brianna couldn't help but feel there was more to Shadowrun Road than met the eye.

2

The truck bumped down a harsh gravel driveway that led to a large farmhouse. It was two stories with a wrap-around porch. Maybe the house had once been beautiful, but now it was in a state of lazy disrepair. The grass hadn't been mowed in what looked like years. Rust collected on the drainage pipes, and old farm machinery sat in a pile on the yard, also covered in weeds. The weathervane atop the house was in danger of toppling over and going through the roof, which already had more than a few shingles missing.

Uncle Shane wasted no time in grabbing Brianna's

suitcase and hauling it up onto the porch. Brianna almost had to run to catch the screen door from closing on her.

Before she entered her temporary home, she looked over her shoulder at the expanse of farmland and the forest of trees beyond the overgrown yard. She heard nothing except the evening wind whistling through the trees and whispering across the blades of tall grass.

Uncle Shane was already turning the football game on the TV when she came through. Her suitcase rested at the bottom of the steps.

"Where's my room?" Brianna asked.

"Up the stairs. Last door on the right," he called, settling into his big easy chair at the center of the room.

Rolling her eyes, Brianna headed up the steps and found her bedroom door. It was a simple room with old, light blue wallpaper and a twin bed that had a patchwork quilt on it. A dresser, a desk, and a nightstand, all made of dark cherrywood, were tucked neatly into corners. With not much to do, Brianna took her time putting away her clothes and setting up her comic books and school supplies on her desk. She'd just finished unpacking when the telephone rang downstairs. The dull roar of the TV quieted, followed by Uncle Shane calling her name up the steps.

"It's your mom!" he bellowed.

Already homesick, Brianna raced down the stairs and grabbed the phone from her uncle. She didn't yet have a cell phone—her mom said she was too young to have one, but she guessed it also had to do with her mom being out of a job for six months. So her uncle's old landline would have to make do while they were separated.

"Mom?" Brianna said, breathless.

"Bree, sweetie!" Mrs. Jenson's bubbly voice exploded over the phone. "Did you have a nice flight? Was there any turbulence? Did they lose your luggage? Have you had dinner yet?"

"Slow down, Mom," Brianna said with a laugh. The warmth of her mother's voice chased away the chills from the disturbing dream and Uncle Shane's cold shoulder. "Yes, no, no, and no, in that order," Brianna said, answering each of her mother's rambling questions.

Mrs. Jenson laughed in return. "Sorry, I'm just . . . you know I didn't like every detail of the master plan, especially where we have to be apart."

Brianna twirled the old curly phone cord in her fingers as she pictured her mother pacing somewhere in Nevada. Her mother was a big worrywart, so if this "master plan" was going to go smoothly, then Brianna needed to give her mother absolutely no reason to worry. That meant nothing but sunshine and rainbows—definitely nothing about terrifying monster cars on creepy roads.

"I know, Mom," Brianna said. "But things will be great."

And she had to hope that wasn't the biggest lie she'd ever told.

∾ ◍ ∾

The wind screamed through the long tunnel of trees. It was not a scream of terror or surprise. It was more a scream of pain. Agony.

Brianna stopped in the middle of the road and looked over her shoulder. There was nothing there. Just broken branches and hundreds upon thousands of dead leaves blown about by the biting autumn wind. Brianna wanted nothing more than to hurry home, but the road was long, and the shadows seemed to get thicker by the second.

Shrieks suddenly echoed through the forest, and Brianna ducked. When nothing fell on her, she craned her neck back to follow the shrill sound. A murder of crows sat in the branches directly above her. Big black birds with glowing red eyes. One of them flapped its wings, hopping onto the next flimsy branch as a few feathers fluttered to the ground like leaves.

The creature opened its mouth and cawed, its screech hitting Brianna in a fresh, icy wave of fear. She stumbled backward and fell to the ground. The cold concrete scraped against her palm and stung. She might be bleeding, but she was too focused on the figure before her to check.

A shadow had appeared at the end of the road, a black silhouette against more darkness. Brianna's breath froze in her chest, unable to get out. The shadow shuffled forward, coming down the road toward Brianna. But its walk was slow and fumbling—as if it was limping. The footsteps came to her like *leaves brushing across pavement. Like bird talons scraping against tree bark.*

Stomp, shhh, shhhh . . .

Finally Brianna's lungs started working again, and her breath rose up in a cloud of steam. Somehow it felt much colder than an autumn day. Colder than even the dead of winter.

Cold like death.

A shiver went down Brianna's spine as the shadowy figure stopped limping and stood at the end of the road.

Then the birds took off overhead and feathers showered down. She lifted her arms to cover her head in case the birds decided they wanted her for dinner instead of a dead animal on the side of the road.

Peeking up at the figure, Brianna watched as it raised its shadowy arm and pointed over Brianna's shoulder.

Brianna couldn't help it: She looked.

∾ 🎃 ∾

Her eyes opened to find a ceiling fan slowly spinning above her. Her heart pounded in her chest like she just ran a race, and even though she had plenty of covers to keep her warm, she'd never felt colder.

Another dream about that road. But unlike last time, she had felt like herself, and it hadn't felt like a memory but more like a—

"Brianna!" Uncle Shane's voice boomed through her door. "Hurry up, or you'll be late!"

Brianna threw back her covers and rushed around her room, getting ready for her first day at her new school. When she finally made it downstairs, Uncle Shane was already eating a bowl of cornflakes and reading a newspaper.

"I'm not driving you to school," Uncle Shane announced as Brianna sat down with her own bowl of cereal.

Brianna shrugged. "Okay."

Uncle Shane hadn't been *mean* to her, really, but he acted as if her existence was a terrible inconvenience. Which, at the very least, was rude.

"You're taking the bus," he said, answering a question Brianna hadn't even asked. "And you'd best get going."

"Where's the bus stop?" Brianna tried not to

sound angry, but he could've told her last night so she'd have set her alarm earlier. She just hoped she wasn't going to be late and miss the bus. She had a feeling he *still* wouldn't drive her even if that happened.

"At the end of the road."

"You mean the end of the driveway?" she asked.

"No, I mean the *road*. You'll have to make it all the way down there. It's about three-quarters of a mile. Better hurry up," he said, taking a sip of his coffee.

Brianna stuffed three more bites of cornflakes into her mouth and grabbed her backpack at the foot of the stairs, then raced out the door.

The morning Pennsylvania air was different than in Texas. For one, it was crisp, not somewhat humid and muggy, and it was chilly even for such an early September day. If Uncle Shane had told her about the bus stop earlier, she would've walked and enjoyed the sunrise coming up through the tees. Instead, she had to run and—when she no longer could—walk fast all the way down the road lined with trees.

By the time she got to the end of the road, the big yellow vehicle was already there, puffing out steam and the brakes whining as if it hated to be stuck in one place too long. Breathless, Brianna caught the door of the bus and heaved herself through.

"Brianna Jenson?" the bus driver, an old man with a shock of white hair and glasses, asked after he glanced at his clipboard.

"Yes . . . sir." Brianna panted.

"Almost left without you," the bus driver said with a frown. "Be sure to get here on time tomorrow, yeah?"

"Yes, sir." Brianna hiked her backpack up her shoulders, ducking her head down to avoid any stares. She quickly found a seat in the back of the bus and stared out the window the entire ride to school.

When she arrived at Drury Gables School, Brianna quickly learned that it was not very big. All grades, kindergarten through twelfth, went to the same school, and even then it felt entirely too small. Brianna had just gone to the office (which was easy to find), and the secretary checked her in and gave her directions to her sixth-grade classroom. The teacher, Mr. Franklin, was nice enough but made just about the biggest mistake you could possibly make as a teacher: He called out the new kid. As if everyone didn't already know she was new!

Mr. Franklin had Brianna stand up in front of the class and introduce herself. She gave as little information as possible ("I'm from Texas and I like art"), then Mr. Franklin pointed to an empty desk toward the back. Brianna sat at the desk and sank low in her seat, hoping to turn invisible for the rest of the morning.

But Mr. Franklin wasn't done yet. When the lunch bell rang, he gestured for Brianna to come to the front.

"Jacob," he called to one of the students, "would you stay a moment, please?"

As the rest of the kids filed out of the classroom for lunch, a boy about Brianna's height with short red hair and a face full of freckles joined her at Mr. Franklin's desk.

"Brianna, this is Jacob Dorham," Mr. Franklin said,

spreading out his arm toward the redheaded kid like he was showing off a trophy. "He's going to show you around the school and answer any questions you might have."

When they were out of earshot of the teacher, Brianna thought about what to say to Jacob. It wasn't that she didn't appreciate the teacher's attempt to help her make friends, but this was awkward. "You don't have to show me around. This school is pretty small."

Jacob shook his head. "It's okay. I'm used to it."

"Why are you used to it?"

"I mean, the teachers ask me to do stuff a lot. My mom's the mayor, so . . ." Jacob shrugged. "Maybe they think I want to"—he made air quotes with his fingers—"'serve the community' just like her."

Brianna wrinkled her nose. "That sounds annoying."

Jacob gave her a smile. "It is."

They walked in silence for a few more steps before Jacob asked, "So are you living with Mr. Jenson? I saw you get on the bus today."

"Yeah, he's my uncle," Brianna said, then quickly added, "it's just for two months, though."

"What's in two months?"

"Mom finishes her job training, and then I go back home."

Jacob was quiet as they turned down the hall toward the cafeteria, then said, "Any chance she'll be done sooner?"

Brianna frowned. It sounded like he wanted to get rid of her quickly. Maybe he resented the fact that he was being made to show her around. After all, he'd just admitted that doing these types of things was *annoying*. Well, that was fine for her.

"I already told you: You don't have to show me around," Brianna snapped. "It's not like I want to be your community service project."

Jacob's mouth popped open. "No, that's not what I—"

Brianna slipped inside the cafeteria before Jacob could say anything else. She didn't need friends in Drury

Gables. She had plenty back home. She'd be just fine on her own.

∞ ⬤ ∞

By the time Brianna dumped her backpack onto the floor of the bus at the end of the day, she was tired and homesick and depressed. She'd just settled into a quiet bus ride home when a boy's face peeked over the seat in front of her.

It was Corey Richter, a student from her class who'd jeered at her for knowing an answer in math that he hadn't.

"You live off Shadowrun Road, right?" Corey asked with a smug grin.

Brianna only then remembered the run-down road sign. "Only for a little while," she replied shortly.

Corey snickered. Then he leaned farther over the seat to whisper menacingly, "So have you seen *her* yet?"

"Shhh, Corey," Kristen, another one of Brianna's classmates, hissed from across the aisle. "You better not let Mr. Garry hear you talking about *her*."

"Who is *her*?" Brianna asked.

"Corey!" Mr. Garry, the bus driver, barked. "Sit down."

Still smirking at Brianna, Corey dropped back onto the seat in front of her. Before Brianna could ask again who this *she* was, it was already her stop at Shadowrun Road. Eager to end this terrible day, she hopped off the bus and faced the road home.

She'd been in such a hurry this morning, she hardly remembered walking through it. But now that the afternoon sun was shining through the dense leaves, it didn't look scary at all. It was nothing like her dreams. In fact, it looked rather ... magical.

It was like a tunnel into a forest with unicorns and elves. She couldn't help but notice how beautiful it all was. The colors of the green leaves in the gold sunlight, their shadows creating a fascinating pattern.

After walking about halfway down Shadowrun Road, Brianna found a lone stump off the side of the street. She didn't have to hurry home because Uncle Shane had told her he sometimes worked late in the evenings. How late that actually was, she wasn't sure, but she suspected she had time to sit down and sketch.

Brianna swept the leaves off the stump and sat down, then pulled out her pencil and notebook and began sketching without any thought at all. It was nice, not having to think and worry. To be caught up in her passion for art. She sketched out the patterns of leaves on the road, and before she knew it, she had filled up three whole pages.

In fact, it wasn't until Brianna felt a tickle at the back of her neck that she even noticed she was still outside. Thinking it was a bug, she swatted at the spot on her neck and returned to her drawing. She could at least finish this sketch before heading home.

But then Brianna felt the tickle again, as if someone was blowing on her skin.

"Stupid bugs," she muttered as she waved around her head with both her hands.

But she saw no fly or gnat.

It was then she realized just how quickly the sun

was setting, the shadows of the trees all around her growing longer and longer.

Suddenly, the hairs on her arms stood and goose bumps decorated her skin as she felt the tickle on her neck once more. But before she could whirl around and look for the source of the weird sensation, her sketchbook was suddenly knocked off her lap and into the leaves at her feet. With a gasp, she reached down to snatch up the book but then felt a pinch on the back of her arm.

Brianna let out a scream, pulling her arm away from whatever pinched her and falling off the stump.

Laughter filled her ears before she managed to pick herself up, and when she did, her vision went red with rage.

"Corey!" she cried. "You jerk!"

Corey stood behind the stump, holding his stomach as he cackled with laughter. "Oh man, you should've seen your face!"

Cheeks red with embarrassment and anger, Brianna stomped her foot. "Just leave me alone!"

Corey's laughter faded into chuckles. "Hey, it's not my fault you didn't hear me. It's not like I was quiet."

"What are you even doing here?" Brianna snapped.

"Cutting across Shadowrun is the best way to get to Jacob's house." Corey pointed in the other direction across the road. "But don't worry, you won't be seeing me on this road for much longer."

Brianna stuffed her sketchbook into her backpack. "And why's that?"

He gave her a cruel smile. "Because *she* will come out soon."

There was that *she* again.

"Who will come out?" Brianna asked.

Corey glanced up and down the road, then gave her another smile. "You'll see. Later, scaredy-cat!"

With that, he hurried across the road and disappeared into the tree line on the other side.

Her good mood now ruined by Corey, Brianna headed down the road to Uncle Shane's farmhouse.

"Uncle Shane?" she called out as she stepped inside the house, but there was no answer.

He must be at work, thought Brianna, though she still wasn't entirely sure what he did for a living. She got a glass of water from the tap, then went upstairs to her room. Without a thought, she opened the door and—

Three...four...*five* big crows sat on various pieces of furniture in her room. Two were on her bed, one was on her desk, another was on her dresser, and one perched on the open window seal.

Brianna screamed, stumbling backward and falling against the hallway wall. Her glass of water hit the carpet and splashed everywhere.

One of the crows on her bed—the largest— hopped from the quilt down to the floor. It tilted its head to the side, blinking its bright red eyes, then clicked its beak and let out a giant screech.

Over the sound echoing in her ears, Brianna could hear footsteps thundering up the stairs. Two seconds later, Uncle Shane burst into the hall and ran to the doorway.

"Shoo! Go on! SCRAM!" he roared, waving his arms and driving the birds out the open window. Cawing and flapping, the crows escaped Brianna's room, leaving a trail of midnight-black feathers in their wake.

When they were all gone, Uncle Shane slammed the window shut and turned back to Brianna. "Kid? Did they hurt ya?"

"N-no," Brianna stuttered, the shock of the birds finally beginning to wear off.

"Well, be more careful next time! Don't leave your window open like that!" Uncle Shane snapped. "And clean up those feathers!" he hollered as he headed back down the stairs.

Brianna said nothing, still trying to stop shaking. But she knew one thing with absolute certainty: Her bedroom window had been closed that morning.

3

Leaves skittered across the asphalt, chased by the autumn wind, while branches creaked and swayed overhead. It made the natural tunnel of trees over Shadowrun Road look alive.

It's too early in the season to be this cold, Brianna thought as she shoved her chilled hands into her well-worn hoodie. But then, she wasn't in Texas anymore, was she?

Today was Friday, which meant it had barely been one full week since she'd come to live in Drury Gables. Life had not gotten any better, but it hadn't really gotten any worse, either. She loved sketching in the afternoons on Shadowrun Road, but today it felt too cold even to hold a pencil.

Brianna's sneakers made an echoing *tap, tap* with every step on the worn asphalt, an occasional *crunch* coming from the dried leaves that decorated the road like the pages of a scrapbook. As she walked, she thought about what she would make for dinner that evening. Tired of eating just sandwiches with deli meat, Brianna had offered to cook that night, and Uncle Shane had merely grunted in response. She'd taken that as a yes.

Since then, she'd been thinking about simple dishes and looking forward to when she could call her mother for cooking advice. It wasn't as if she needed an excuse to call, but it was something to talk about. Focusing on things like oven temperatures and ingredients meant her mother probably wouldn't notice that she hadn't made a single friend, and that most of her days were incredibly lonely. Mrs. Jenson was stressed enough with the training

program. She didn't need to worry about Brianna not getting along well at school.

Brianna was so wrapped up in thinking about
tonight's spaghetti dinner that it took her a long time to
realize that the echo of her footsteps seemed to bounce
back to her twice.

Tap. Tap. Tap.

She tilted her head with a frown, hearing the echo
return for a fourth time. Echoes weren't supposed to do
that. They faded. They didn't come back stronger than
before.

The leaves continued to roll across the road,
and the wind blew harder, creating a whistle through the
trees that almost sounded, to Brianna's ears, like a person
whistling. The wind blew again, and the branches trembled. It whipped Brianna's ponytail around and batted it
against her cheek. As she pulled down her hair, Brianna
realized the sound of the wind sounded more like a soft
scream instead. It reminded her of something, but she
couldn't remember what.

Shivering, Brianna looked over her shoulder. The sun was lower in the sky, outlining the branches completely black against the orange glow of the sun. She bit her lip and turned back around, walking faster this time.

Tap. Tap. Tap. Tap. TAP. TAP.

Brianna stopped, her heart pounding. The echo was so loud now. No, she could no longer deny it. It wasn't an echo; those were actual, *real* footsteps behind her. Gripping the straps of her backpack until her knuckles turned white, she picked up the pace, almost running down Shadowrun Road.

TaptaptaptaptaptapTAPTAPTAP.

Brianna whirled around.

There was no one.

Panting, Brianna scanned the line of trees on either side. From right to left, she searched the lone road, just standing there and shivering in the cold wind.

The road was empty. Not even a squirrel, raccoon, possum, deer, or stray dog in sight. But even if she had seen an animal amid the pile of leaves or darting between the trees, deep down she would've known that those had been *human* footsteps.

Clear as day. Following right behind her. Getting louder.

Brianna held her breath, trying to slow her racing heart. This was so silly! There was no one on this road, and even if there had been, she would've heard all the crunching of dead leaves if they'd run into the forest. The underbrush was too thick for even the most light-footed creature to scamper across unheard.

"Who...who's there?" she tried, her voice soft against the sound of the wind whirling through the trees, over and under the branches. Her words were practically drowned out.

No one responded. No one stepped out from behind the trees.

That's when she remembered Corey Richter's cruel prank. Though she hadn't seen him on Shadowrun Road since then, that didn't mean he wouldn't come back for more "fun."

"Corey!" she cried. "Come out! I know it's you!" Her voice was louder this time, causing a real echo to bounce from tree to tree, fading with each repetition.

His words from that day came back to her: *"But don't worry, you won't be seeing me on this road for much longer. Because* she *will come out soon."*

Pressing her lips together, Brianna turned and was relieved to see the turnoff to Uncle Shane's driveway. It wasn't very far at all—she could make it.

Make it from *what*, though?

The wind?

This mysterious *she* whom Corey had mentioned earlier?

Brianna shook her head. She was being ridiculous. A big scaredy-cat. Corey had just been trying to scare her. Besides, each night this week she'd sat on the side of the road, sketching until it was almost dark and she couldn't see her drawing anymore. This was her safe haven, her one peaceful place between her grouchy uncle and the bullies at school.

She wouldn't let some stupid tapping and a mean boy ruin that for her.

So she started walking again, forcing her steps to maintain a steady, normal pace. She wasn't afraid. There was nothing there to be afraid of. *There's nothing there at all.*

But the footsteps started once again. *Tap. Tap. Tap. Tap. Tap.*

They were close now—so close that Brianna felt like the footsteps were about to tread on her heels. She kept going, but the footsteps came just as quickly. So quickly that she fully expected the back of her heel to be stepped on by someone's toes.

Tap. Tap. Tap. Tap. Tap.

"Leave. Me. ALONE!" Brianna shouted at no one.

Unable to stand it any longer, Brianna started running. Her backpack bounced up and down against her spine and shoulders. She ran, and for a moment she felt relief—there was only the sound of her own feet, and her own breathing, and her own racing pulse.

Then the hairs on her arms and the back of her

neck stood at attention, prickling painfully as the pounding footsteps came after her, loud and fast, as if they were angry, chasing her down and coming up behind her like a speeding train. Fear—cold and dark—wrapped around Brianna's throat and squeezed. She ran faster and faster, but the footsteps kept up, always just one beat behind her.

TAP. TAP. TAPTAPTAPTAPTAP.

Brianna gave a shout in fear as the footsteps seemed to be right on top of her. The next second she practically leaped onto Uncle Shane's driveway. The minute her feet left the road, the steps stopped and the sound cut off like a heavy door had slammed behind her. Brianna was so surprised at the sudden silence that she chanced a look over her shoulder.

No one was there. The road was empty, save for a few leaves tumbling and toppling over one another.

Brianna wasn't sure if this was worse or not. She'd be just as scared if an actual person really *had* been there chasing her down. But invisible footsteps were hardly better.

Still spooked, Brianna didn't want to slow her pace. She ran all the way down Uncle Shane's long, long driveway and up the porch, ripping open the screen door and bursting into the warm living room that smelled of woodsmoke.

"What the—*You!*" Shane jerked up from his armchair, startled at the way Brianna had crashed into the living room like a tornado.

He stepped around the chair and gestured at his shirt, a wet stain all down his chest. He shook a Coke can at her. "Look what you made me do, kid!" he snarled. "Scared me half to death bursting in like that. I spilled my drink down my favorite shirt!"

But Brianna barely heard him. "Someone was chasing me!"

Uncle Shane's eyebrows shot up. "Chasing you? What'd they look like?"

Brianna opened and closed her mouth a few times, her heartbeat at last beginning to slow. Here in the living room with the soft light, the crackling fire, and the warmth, what she had seen—or *not* seen, rather—seemed absolutely impossible. How could she tell her uncle that she had been chased by...no one?

"Well? Come on!" he urged, striding toward the door and pulling it open. Brianna hugged her arms and peered outside along with her uncle, even though she knew the yard would be empty.

She took a deep breath. "I was...I was walking from the bus stop and I heard footsteps behind me. But I turned around and...and no one was there."

Uncle Shane's brow furrowed. "Then you were imagining it, kid," he grumbled as he closed the door.

"No, no, I wasn't! The footsteps got *louder*, Uncle Shane!"

"There can't be any chasing if no one is there to do the chasing," Uncle Shane said, walking to the kitchen and scrubbing irritably at his wet shirt, as if the matter was settled.

"But—" Brianna protested, the fear still gripping her tight. If only she could convince him there really was

41

something there, he might be willing to pick her up from school instead of forcing her to take the bus home.

Just then, the phone rang. Giving Brianna another strange look, Uncle Shane walked over to answer the phone. "Hello? Yeah . . . yeah, she's here. One second." He placed one hand over the receiver and turned back to Brianna. "It's your mom."

Uncle Shane held out the phone to her and the invitation was clear: *Do you want to tell your mother about the invisible person chasing you?* No. No, she didn't. There was no way she could say something so bizarre without her mother worrying and asking a hundred questions.

Swallowing down all the panic that had come from her walk home, Brianna took the phone. "Hi, Mom."

"Bree! It's so good to hear your voice. Today was brutal." Mrs. Jenson sounded tired but warm and affectionate. Brianna wished she could take her voice and make a blanket out of it, wrapping herself up in the comfort that it brought every time she talked.

"Really? What happened?" For a brief instant,

Brianna had a sliver of hope. Maybe her mother hated the training program. Maybe she could go home now. The next instant, she felt bad for even thinking that. She *wanted* her mother to finally find a job that made her happy. That made her come home feeling empowered and satisfied.

"Oh, just some complicated computer software we had to learn today. But I'm actually pretty good at it. What about your day, sweetie? How was school?"

"It's great, Mom," Brianna lied. Unfortunately, it was becoming much too easy to lie to her mother lately, and Brianna had never lied to her mother before all this. But if she *didn't* lie, that would mean telling the truth, and if Brianna told the truth, her mom would hop on the first plane out of Nevada, pick her up, and all their plans would be ruined.

"Well, that's wonderful, Bree. I'm glad you're enjoying it up there. From what I remember, it was a quiet little town. I liked living there, that is ... until your father passed away. Then we needed a change."

Over the past week, Brianna had tried to remember more of Drury Gables, but the memories were few and far between. Occasionally, she would remember brief moments of walking down Shadowrun Road, but she couldn't tell if they were memories from her own past or from her dreams.

Her dreams!

Brianna clapped her hand over her mouth. She'd totally forgotten about the strange dreams she'd had when she first arrived in Pennsylvania and the chill and fear that had come with them. Were her dreams and those invisible footsteps somehow related? After all, they were connected through the road. That couldn't be a coincidence . . . could it?

"Bree?"

Her mom's voice pulled her to the present, and she tried to refocus. "Um, what?"

"I asked if you needed help with dinner tonight."

"Oh . . . oh! Um, yeah." Brianna pulled out her notebook to take notes as her mother explained how to cook the meatballs and prepare the buttery spread for the garlic toast.

When Mrs. Jenson was done with her instructions, she stopped and said, "You know, Bree . . . I want you to know that I'm really proud of you."

A sudden burning sensation started in the back of Brianna's eyes and throat. Grumpy uncles, bullies at schools, no friends, creepy roads with invisible feet . . . It was all worth it to hear those words from her mom. Brianna had to steady her voice to reply, "I'm proud of you, too, Mom."

4

School continued to be terrible—the exact opposite of what Brianna had to keep telling her mother. She was teased for being a know-it-all when she happened to know the right answer. It wasn't *her* fault that she'd already read the book they were studying in English. But it *was* her fault at gym class when she couldn't pass the ball to her teammates and missed the basket several times. They all booed her off the court, and with her face hot, she disappeared to hide in a bathroom stall the rest of the game. Coach Higgins never even went looking for her.

Not only that, but on the bus ride home, Brianna

worried about the disembodied footsteps. With each day that passed where nothing happened, she became more convinced that it had to have been her imagination or Corey Richter somehow playing another prank on her, though he hadn't owned up to it.

Still, she didn't like riding the bus. Corey and Kristen sat behind her and whispered cruel things about her superhero shirt and gray hoodie with Sharpie doodles.

On Wednesday morning, Brianna worked up the courage to ask her uncle a question she'd been wondering for a while. "Why can't you drive me home from school?"

Uncle Shane glanced up from his paper and fixed Brianna with an annoyed look. "I don't usually get home from work until six in the evening and you can't wait at school for two hours for me to come get you."

"Where do you work?" Brianna asked, thinking that she might be able to wait for him at his office while he worked. She'd waited at her mom's office plenty of times.

"The auto repair shop in town. I fix cars…and farm equipment," he answered shortly, taking a sip of his very black coffee. And, as if reading her mind, he added, "It's no place for kids. There's a lot of dangerous tools around there, and I don't want you getting into any trouble."

"I wouldn't get into any trouble."

"The answer is no." Uncle Shane stood from his table. "We're shorthanded at the shop, and there's a lot of cars and tractors to be fixed. I can't worry about you while I work on large machinery. Understood?"

"Yes, sir," Brianna said glumly, and went back to stirring brown sugar into her oatmeal.

∽ 🎃 ∽

Friday rolled around, and Brianna looked forward to two whole days without classmates. Plus, the mid-September afternoon had even warmed up a bit. The sun wasn't too low in the sky, and the wind was rather mild. And after five whole days of no spooky footsteps, she'd written the whole thing off as her imagination.

She was free to sit and sketch on a beautiful autumn afternoon.

Excited at the prospect, Brianna felt her steps lighten, and she even hummed a little tune to herself as she started down Shadowrun Road. She couldn't remember the name of the tune, but she knew it was one she'd learned in primary school, years ago. Without realizing it, she allowed herself to get carried away with the melody.

A third of the way to her stump, she could've sworn someone else was humming with her. Immediately, she stopped and swallowed hard. She didn't want to think about the footsteps again.

That never happened.

Regardless, she walked a little faster, her sneakers crunching the dry leaves as her gaze swept across the road.

The black concrete was worn and cracked with age, baked by the sun that shone in the rare spots where the trees thinned. The leaves moved and flowed with the wind like seashells tossed on the shore by waves. Trees that lined the road glowed a soft copper with the sunlight stretching through the tunnel of branches.

It really was a lovely fall day.

Then there was the smell. Fall. Autumn. Crisp, with a faint hint of pumpkins. Brianna felt the tension lift off her shoulders, and she smiled as the leaves were picked up by a rowdy breeze and tossed into the air. Twirling like they were caught in the dance of the Sugar Plum Fairy.

Finally, Brianna came to the stump off the side of the road. Sweeping her hand across the wood rings, she brushed away the leaves and sat down, pulling her feet up into a cross-legged position. She tugged off her backpack and pulled out her notebook and began sketching.

At first, the sketch was just a doodle, simply letting her pencil roam free and easy across the lined paper. She drew a lightning bolt and then a starship and then a wizard's hat and a knight's sword. She doodled a dragon breathing fire up into the holes of the notebook paper.

Then she started on a blank page and began sketching a landscape. It was a field with a tractor and a scarecrow, and a barn off in the distance. The scene looked familiar to her somehow, but she couldn't remember from when . . . or where.

Could it have been a place she'd once known from her time in Drury Gables as a child?

She sketched the field of wheat and shaded the stalks to depict the shadows and the position of the sun. Remembering how Mrs. Brinks had taught her that the position of light was important when drawing shadows.

Halfway through drawing the tractor, Brianna realized she was humming again. How long had she been drawing, anyway? Feeling like she needed a break, Brianna flexed her fingers and lifted her head back to relieve the tension in her neck from staring down at the paper too long.

She froze.

At the end of the tunnel of trees was a small figure backlit against the setting sun. Brianna's breath stalled in her chest, and she only then noticed just how chilly it had gotten. The biting cold was back, nipping at her fingers gripping the pencil.

The figure didn't move, far off in the distance. Brianna squinted, trying to make out more of its features, her heart bumping and thumping in her chest. Immediately, Brianna thought about those footsteps.

But those footsteps were never there, Brianna reminded herself. She had to stop thinking about it or her imagination would run away with her just like it did that day. Swallowing hard, she glanced down at her sketch, and when she looked back up...

The figure was gone.

Nothing at the end of the road, at the far end of the tunnel of trees.

Brianna let out a heavy sigh. "See? Just a trick of the shadows," she said out loud, wanting to hear her own voice in the silence of the surrounding woods. *I'll just finish this sketch and pack up.*

But the shadowy figure at the end of the road had freaked her out so much that her creative spirit was gone.

She couldn't produce any art when she was so shaken up like that.

On second thought, I'll leave now.

Brianna lifted her head and let out a squeak of terror.

A young girl stood in the middle of the road. She was close enough for Brianna to make out her orange dress with a cream ribbon sash and shiny black shoes. The little girl's light brown curls hung above her shoulders and didn't move in the teasing breeze.

Brianna was shocked. Where had this girl come from? It was as if she had appeared out of nowhere.

Had *she* been the figure at the end of the tunnel? No, that couldn't be right, either. That was impossible—to move from all that way so fast.

"Hello?" she called to the girl.

The girl didn't move.

Brianna's pencil slipped from her stiff fingers into the leaves at the base of the stump. Her hands were freezing! When had it gotten so cold?

Fear creeping up her spine like a black widow spider, Brianna stooped down to grab her pencil. It only took her a few seconds to find it, but when she straightened back up...the mysterious girl was no longer there.

Brianna gasped and leaped to her feet, clutching her notebook to her chest, and turned all around, searching for the girl. She couldn't have gotten far. Brianna had looked away for less than five seconds! And yet, Shadowrun Road was completely empty.

Brianna was still looking around when another sound made her jump. It was the caw of a crow. When she looked up, she caught sight of several of the black birds moving through the dense branches of the forest. The creatures reminded her of the time when they had invaded her room, and then again in her dream. Another of their cries pierced the air, and Brianna cringed.

Wanting no more of creepy crows, shadowy figures, invisible footsteps, or disappearing girls, Brianna grabbed her backpack, scattering leaves onto the road and into the wind. She shoved her notebook and pencil inside and started jogging, eager to get home.

While Brianna hurried down the road, Corey's mysterious threat came back to her once again: *"Because she will come out soon."*

Was this her—the little girl in the orange dress? What did that mean? Where were her parents?

In record time, Brianna turned off the road onto the long driveway, and as she did so, she stepped into a pile of orange gunk.

"Eww," Brianna groaned, hopping on one foot to inspect the stuff on her shoe.

In the end it was the smell that gave it away: a pumpkin.

Smashed, rotting pumpkin now covered the bottom of Brianna's sneaker. Wrinkling her nose, she tried her best to wipe it off in the dried grass, but only large chunks came off. With a sigh, she continued up the driveway, imagining the anger that Uncle Shane would have if she tracked smelly pumpkin into the house. But she didn't want to spend any more time near the road trying to wipe off the stuff.

By the time she got to the porch, Brianna remembered that there was a water spigot at the back of the house. Circling around, Brianna pushed up the sleeves of her hoodie and turned on the water, washing the pumpkin off her sneaker with care.

It was only then that she noticed she wasn't as cold as she'd been before. Which was odd, considering the sun was much lower in the sky now and the evening chill had settled across the fields.

Flicking water off her hands and shaking her shoe, Brianna promised herself that this afternoon would be the last time she ever sketched on Shadowrun Road.

5

The girl on Shadowrun Road had occupied much of Brianna's thoughts over the weekend and well into the following week. So much, in fact, that Brianna bombed her history pop quiz on Monday and missed the teacher calling on her twice. Corey Richter had wasted no time in pelting her with little chunks of eraser with the excuse that he was helping her pay attention. But even Corey's taunting couldn't distract her from the image of the girl standing on the road.

The girl had looked to be no more than nine or ten. So it wasn't as if she was a toddler wandering around the woods, but still. What child can just appear and dis-appear without making a sound in the middle of all those leaves and branches? It didn't make sense.

More than once, Brianna considered asking Corey about the girl, but her pride wouldn't let her. She simply didn't want to see Corey's glee that he'd scared her so much that she was actually frightened of a younger kid.

The entire week, she looked for the girl on the road again, but each afternoon, it was just Brianna, the leaves, trees, and wind. As the bus pulled away from the Drury Gables School parking lot on Friday, Brianna was once again obsessing over the girl. Maybe the girl went to the school but was in a younger grade. Or maybe she even lived close to Shadowrun Road. There were so many unanswered questions swirling around her head that Brianna barely noticed the kids getting off at their stops. She also hadn't noticed how much darker the sky seemed to be getting. At this hour, the field of wheat that they passed was usually bathed in gold—bright, cheerful, and beautiful. Now it was half covered in shadow. The changing of seasons was upon them.

That meant Shadowrun Road might be much darker, too, so Brianna decided to get some of her questions answered. At least knowing more about this mysterious girl might help put Brianna's mind at ease on the lonely walk home. But she still refused to give Corey the satisfaction of knowing he'd spooked her so much.

Luckily, Brianna had chosen a seat directly behind Jacob Dorham. Brianna hadn't spoken to Jacob since the time she'd told him she didn't want to be his community service project. It felt awkward to talk to him after that, so she'd avoided him when she could. And though she still had no desire to be his friend, he might at least be able to fulfill his duties as her guide. Besides, he was the one student in class who didn't seem to be outright mean or cold toward her.

Brianna leaned over the seat in front of her and whispered, *"Pssst."*

Jacob glanced behind him, and his eyebrows shot up onto his forehead. "Hey."

"I was wondering . . . um . . ." she fumbled, attempting to keep her voice low over the chattering throughout the bus.

"Wondering about what?" Jacob said.

"Are there any other kids who live around where I live—around Shadowrun Road, I mean?" Brianna asked.

"No . . ." Jacob's brow furrowed. "A few families used to live off the road, but they moved away, and now it's mostly just farmland around it. My house is the closest. Why?"

"I bet you she saw her," came a harsh whisper.

Brianna and Jacob both turned toward the source: Corey Richter, leaning across the aisle, clearly eavesdropping.

A sinking feeling started in the pit of Brianna's stomach while goose bumps erupted down her arms. She really didn't want to admit it to Corey, but she couldn't stop thinking about the girl. "Who is she?"

"The most famous girl in all Drury Gables," Corey said, grinning from ear to ear.

Kristen, who had also apparently been eavesdropping, turned around in her bus seat and glared at him. "We're not supposed to talk about her."

Corey rolled his eyes. "What, are you going to tell on me, Kristen? Don't be such a Goody Two-shoes. If Brianna really saw her, don't you think she should know what kind of danger she's in?"

Danger? From a little girl? He had to be trying to scare her! "What are you talking about?" Brianna snapped.

"Brianna!" Mr. Garry shouted, making Brianna jump. "Sit yerself down."

Her face hot, Brianna lowered herself into her seat. Too embarrassed at being called out, Brianna pulled out a book from her backpack and attempted to read it, avoiding eye contact with both Jacob and Corey. But she could barely concentrate on it. She had read the same paragraph four times before she gave up and stuffed the book inside her backpack. She shivered and gripped the straps of her backpack tightly, her thumbnail absent-mindedly scraping along its threads. The trees grew thicker, and she knew they were nearing her stop at the edge of the woods off Shadowrun Road.

When the bus slowed, its loud brakes creaking and squealing, Brianna got up and tried to clear her head. She hadn't seen the girl for a week, or heard the footsteps, so there shouldn't be anything to worry about today, either.

But Brianna wasn't convinced.

As she passed Jacob, she could feel his eyes on her, but she didn't look back at him. She didn't want him to see the fear that must have been all over her face.

"It's darker than it was yesterday." Mr. Garry nodded toward the tunnel of trees bordering Shadowrun as Brianna walked down the bus steps. "You be careful down that road." Brianna was already off the bus when Mr. Garry gave her a deep-set frown of obvious worry and added in a low, sinister voice, "*Very* careful."

Before Brianna had a chance to ask him what he meant, Mr. Garry had already pulled the lever and the bus door squeaked closed. The brakes creaked, and the bus rolled forward, letting out a puff of exhaust smoke that made Brianna step back and wrinkle her nose.

She stood there watching the bus turn around the bend in the trees and out of sight, driving down the next mile to Jacob's stop. The breeze picked up just then and wove through the branches, making them creak like the brakes of the bus and whistle like a teakettle boiling over.

With a shiver, Brianna hunched her shoulders and zipped up her hoodie all the way, burying her chin into the fabric's warm folds. She could still smell her mother's favorite fabric softener and was strangely glad that Uncle Shane was so bad at doing laundry.

Taking a deep breath, she started down the road under the canopy of branches. Her feet moved quickly across the dark pavement, and as usual, Shadowrun Road was vacant. She'd walked down this road for three weeks, every morning and every afternoon, and she had never seen a car. It was as if no one in Drury Gables cared to venture this far away from the edge of town.

The last rays of the sun reached only a third of the

way down the road before the darkness took over completely. The second Brianna's other foot left the last bit of light, the cold seemed to consume her. It seeped through her clothes and clung to her skin like fog, thick and damp and heavy. A whole tremor ripped through Brianna's spine, and her body shook with a jerk.

Brianna walked faster.

Someone else started walking, too.

Brianna let out a tiny sound that was somehow between a gasp and a groan, a sound of fear and dread. The footsteps were back. Even though she knew what she would see—nothing—she couldn't help it. She turned, her eyes scoured hungrily for *any*body—a shadowy figure, Corey, Jacob, Uncle Shane, a stray dog . . . *the girl in the orange dress*. But the road was empty, save for the piles of dead leaves and fallen twigs poking out of the underbrush.

Brianna walked as fast as she could toward Uncle Shane's house without running. If she ran, then the footsteps might start running, too, and she didn't want to be chased again. She might not get away this time.

And she still had so far to go...

Even with her blood pounding in her ears, Brianna could hear the footsteps loud and clear behind her own, only this time there was something different about them.

Before, they had been tapping, light, and energetic—a bit like a child's footsteps. Not like the angry, heavy clomping of an adult's footsteps, like Uncle Shane's or even the high-heeled click of Mrs. Brinks, her art teacher back in Richland.

In fact, the footsteps had been a lot like Brianna's, but today they weren't.

The footsteps were uneven. One foot stomping against the pavement and the other shuffling and dragging through the leaves with a loud whisper.

It was more like *STOMP, shhh, shhh. STOMP, shhh, shhh.*

The sound reminded Brianna of the time she had broken her right foot on a field trip to a state park and had to lean on a friend all the way back to the bus.

She had relied heavily on her left foot and dragged her broken one behind her, favoring it.

The other thing it reminded her of? Zombies.

She'd seen a spooky movie once where the undead creatures with pale faces, white eyes, and gaping mouths stretched their hands out and dragged their feet, shuffling and groaning, hungry for brains.

Brianna now wished she had never seen such a movie. Could that be what was after her? A *zombie*?

Brianna checked over her shoulder, her heart pounding harder and harder, furious in her chest. There was nothing behind her, just like the times before. The branches trembled and waved in the late-September wind and their sound was a soft scream—like a real human scream.

More than ever before, Brianna was reminded of her dream. It actually felt like she was in the dream again. Hearing the wind and seeing the shadows grow with each step, she half expected more crows to suddenly appear with their scary red eyes and haunting shrieks.

Brianna's hands trembled, but the footsteps had suddenly stopped. She looked back and found no one there yet again. No one to come after her. No one to drag her into the darkness of the surrounding woods.

She could just stay here and watch the dark and walk backward. Maybe if she walked backward, the footsteps would never return.

But just as she thought that, they started up again—*STOMP, shhh, shhh. STOMP, shhh, shhh*—coming toward her quick!

With a whimper, Brianna took off running. As she ran, the dragging feet hurried after her. Faster. Inhuman. No person with an injured foot could go so fast.

Brianna opened her mouth to scream for help, but she couldn't. No sound came out, and a gust of cold air tickled her throat and made it dry. Leaves picked up in the wild wind, and the branches hit against one another, whistling, screaming, and beating.

STOMP, shhh, shhh. STOMP, shhh, shhh. STOMP, shhh, shhh. STOMP, shhh, shhh.

Her lungs felt like they were about to burst, and her feet felt like they were going to fall off. She couldn't run down the whole road like this, but she was getting closer. Meanwhile, the dragging feet were gaining on her with every step.

Unbeknownst to Brianna, her shoestring came loose as she ran, and she tripped on it, causing her to fall onto the side of the road and into a large pile of leaves.

Leaves flew up, tossed into the wind like a mini tornado.

Just as Brianna was flailing about, attempting to get up, headlights swung into view at the end of the tunnel. The car revved its engine as it raced down the dark tunnel of Shadowrun Road, casting bright yellow beams across the black asphalt.

Brianna gasped—not at the car or its speed but at the image within its headlights: Standing in the middle of the road was the girl in the orange dress.

Brianna had been able to see her only because she was illuminated by the car's high beams. Her body was ... translucent, somehow. The yellow lights shone right through her.

Was this girl ... a ghost?

The girl stared at Brianna with a hateful, sour expression as the car came upon her, closer and closer.

Brianna screamed, ducking her face into her hands as the car ran right through the girl. But when Brianna looked back up, the girl was gone.

Gasping and wheezing, Brianna stared at the car as it rounded the bend, its red taillights flashing out of view. She looked back at the spot in the road, and it was vacant.

No girl.

No ghost.

Her face wet with tears of terror, Brianna picked herself out of the leaves and ran the last bit of the road and all the way down Uncle Shane's driveway.

She stepped inside the house, panting, trembling. Her hands were shaking so bad that she could barely turn the lock behind her.

"Hey, kid!" Uncle Shane leaned out of the kitchen with a fierce scowl. "Don't slam doors and hurry it up. Your mother is on the phone for you," he said. "I've got her on hold. Make it snappy—I'm hungry."

Numb, Brianna dropped her backpack on the rug and walked to the kitchen, taking the phone from her uncle. He either didn't notice her red eyes and pale face, or he didn't care.

"H-hello?" she croaked into the phone.

"Bree? Sweetheart? Are you all right? You sound just terrible."

"M-Mom, I—" Brianna let out a whimper and a hiccup and was just about to spill her guts about everything that had happened when she caught herself.

So what if there's a ghost haunting the road? What can Mom do about it? She could come get you and take you away from this miserable, lonely, haunted place, a little, selfish voice inside Brianna's head argued.

But then it would be her mom miserable for a long time instead of Brianna miserable for just over a month.

Swallowing back her unbelievable story, and her fears and complaints, and the truth, Brianna cleared her throat and tried her best fake, cheerful voice. "I'm fine, Mom!"

"Are you sure?" her mother pressed. "You sounded like you were about to cry. What happened?"

Brianna bit her bottom lip, searching her mind for a believable lie. "I'm just out of breath. I was playing a game of tag with a friend."

So far, Brianna hadn't talked about friends in an effort to avoid more lies, except she couldn't see a way around it this time.

But it achieved the desired effect—her mom's tone changed immediately. "A friend? Who is it?"

"Jacob Dorham," Brianna answered without thinking.

"Dorham . . . Hmm, that name sounds familiar."

"His mom is the mayor."

"Oh, that's right!" her mother exclaimed excitedly. "I remember that family. You know, I used to see

Mrs. Dorham sometimes when I picked you up from day care. She'd been picking up her son, then, too. Is he nice?"

It took Brianna a second to realize her mother was referring to Jacob. "Oh yeah, he's nice."

"Does he own a cat? Is that why you're sniffling?"

Sighing, Brianna sat down on a kitchen chair to rest her aching legs. "No, Mom, he doesn't have a cat."

"Because you know you're allergic."

"I know," Brianna said, shaking her head at her mother's incessant worrying. And that was over an innocent cat . . . what would she say if she knew it was a ghost?

"Well, I'm glad you have a friend, honey."

If Jacob actually *was* her friend, then he could've told Brianna the story behind this ghost. At least now she understood why Corey had been so mysterious and spooky when he'd talked about the "she" on Shadowrun Road—he'd been referring to a *ghost.* Clearly there was more going on here than her classmates were willing to admit, but how could she talk to her mom about that without making her worry?

"Mom, do you know what other families used to live along Shadowrun Road?"

Mrs. Jenson was silent for a moment, before she said, "You mean besides us?"

Brianna remembered Uncle Shane telling her that she'd once lived off Shadowrun—not that she knew exactly where. "Yeah. Like, any other families with kids?"

"Not that I know of, but the house your father and I bought had been vacant for years. And there were already a few houses that had been sold off for farmland. Why do you ask, sweetheart?"

Not wanting to make her mother any more curious, Brianna hurriedly replied, "Jacob had said something and I was just wondering, that's all. So... how was your day?"

Brianna hardly listened as her mother gushed about her latest management training course. All she could hear was that sound echoing in her head:

STOMP, shhh, shhh . . .

6

I'm walking home with a ghost.

That was the first thing Brianna thought when she woke up the next morning.

As she got dressed and made herself and her uncle a few pieces of toast with grape jelly and butter, Brianna wondered why it was that she'd started seeing this ghost—or why it had only now decided to show itself. What had changed?

She thought back to each of the strange encounters. The footsteps, the girl appearing and disappearing, and then the ghost in the headlights. Maybe there was a pattern.

That's when Brianna realized: It happened on a Friday. Each time, it had been a Friday afternoon on her way home from school. Three times in a row—that was a pattern, wasn't it? What she was to do with this revelation, she wasn't sure, but it was somewhat reassuring to have discovered a clue about this mysterious haunting.

Over the weekend, she tried to keep herself busy. She even asked her uncle if he needed help with any chores. But Uncle Shane just shooed her away and then disappeared for the bulk of the day. He'd mentioned something about going to the barn and working, but he'd been in a rush, so Brianna hadn't asked about it further. Maybe Uncle Shane liked to farm on the side. She even daydreamed that maybe he had horses in his barn and he'd let her ride one eventually. It was silly, though. Even if he had horses, he probably wouldn't let her ride one.

As the weekend went by, Brianna found other

ways to keep herself busy. She sketched, watched cartoons, and fixed meals. But by the time Monday rolled around, she could no longer ignore what lay ahead. Another week, and another Friday.

Brianna considered asking Uncle Shane about it. After all, he'd been living off Shadowrun for years and years. Surely he had to have seen the ghost? But then, he'd never been forced to walk down the whole road every Friday afternoon. And even if he had seen the girl, he might have thought she was just that—a girl, not a ghost, like Brianna had at first. Uncle Shane was also the kind of person who didn't seem to believe in anything, especially the supernatural.

Still, Brianna felt like she had to talk to *someone* about it. Her friends back home would be nice to talk to, but it's not like they'd actually be able to help her—they were over a thousand miles away!

She couldn't tell her mother, Uncle Shane, nor any of her friends back in Richland, so who could she tell?

The only person Brianna felt comfortable talking

to was Jacob Dorham. He might not exactly *want* to talk to her, but if he was her guide at school, then he could be her guide to Drury Gables, too.

So, on Monday, in their class right before lunch, Brianna found her chance to talk to Jacob. Now that they were done reading *Where the Red Fern Grows*, Mr. Franklin had a bunch of the old books that needed to be taken back to the library. As usual, Mr. Franklin had picked Jacob for the task, who had accepted it without complaint, though Brianna was sure he'd much rather head straight to the cafeteria with the rest of his friends.

But this was her chance to talk to Jacob alone.

Brianna's hand shot into the air. "I can help Jacob, Mr. Franklin."

Mr. Franklin blinked behind his horn-rimmed glasses. "Well, that's very kind of you, Brianna. Why don't you take the other stack here?"

Brianna felt Jacob's eyes on her as she hurried to the front of the class and scooped up the stack of books. Silently, the two kids headed out of the classroom and turned left down the long hallway toward the library. Their steps echoed, bouncing off the metal lockers and clanging in her ears. She was reminded of the footsteps on Shadowrun Road, and she tried to suppress a shiver.

"Um," Brianna started in a small voice, "about what Corey said on Friday..."

Jacob frowned, his walk picking up speed. "I don't remember."

Brianna swallowed. She really should have rehearsed this conversation earlier. "Well, he called her the most famous girl in Drury Gables. Who was he talking about?"

At that, Jacob stopped completely, his face draining of color to a ghostly white. He glanced around and licked his lips. "You know Corey. You shouldn't believe anything that he says."

"But Kristen knows about her, too! Anyway, I think he was right. I did see—"

"Brianna," Jacob cut her off. "I already told you that no one lives around Shadowrun Road except you and your uncle." Then he balanced the stack of books under one arm and pulled open the library door. Brianna hadn't even noticed they'd already arrived.

"Exactly!" she said, following him inside. "No one *lives* there."

Jacob crossed to the library counter, set down the stack of books, and pressed a finger to his lips. "Shhhhh!"

Ignoring his warning, Brianna set down her stack next to his and faced him, hands on her hips. "Jacob, I hear footsteps behind me, but when I turn around, there's no one there. And I *have* seen the girl Corey was talking about—the little girl in an orange dress."

Fear flashed across Jacob's face, confirming that Brianna's mind wasn't playing tricks on her after all. There really *was* something out there, and Jacob knew it, too.

"Is Shadowrun Road haunted?" It was Brianna's first time saying it out loud, and she didn't like how scared she sounded.

Jacob took a step back. "We shouldn't be talking about this."

"Why?" Brianna demanded. "What happened on that road? What happened to that girl in the orange dress?" With every question, Brianna's voice grew louder and louder. "She's a ghost—I know she is. I saw *through* her body!"

Just then, a clatter came from the back of the stacks, and Jacob and Brianna both whirled around to find none other than Kristen emerge from behind a bookshelf. Without a glance at Brianna or Jacob, Kristen ran out of the library. She didn't even bother to check out her books.

"Great," Jacob muttered under his breath. "Now you've done it."

Brianna crossed her arms and scowled. "Done what?"

Jacob shook his head and didn't answer. Instead, he headed out of the library, too, leaving Brianna alone to worry about not only the ghost haunting her but what she had supposedly done.

∽ 🎃 ∽

Brianna ended up finding out during her final class. A knock sounded at the door, and the entire class looked up from their notebooks, eager to find out who might be going home early.

A high school student aide came in. Brianna had seen the girl with curly blond hair and braces in the office when she'd gotten her class schedule on her very first day. "Mr. Franklin, Brianna Jenson needs to come to the principal's office."

Brianna's jaw dropped as her cheeks and neck heated with embarrassment. Why her? What had she done? As the rest of the kids broke out in whispers, Brianna slid low in her seat, hoping to disappear entirely.

"Thank you, Stephanie. Does she need to pack her things?" Mr. Franklin asked the student aide.

"Yessir," Stephanie replied.

Mr. Franklin turned away from his whiteboard and frowned at Brianna. "All right, Brianna, you better get moving." He nodded toward the door.

In shocked silence, Brianna picked up her things and shouldered her backpack, her face burning. Why the principal's office? What had she done that was so wrong? She ignored Jacob's stare and Kristen's smirk.

She'd never been sent to the principal's office before. She imagined telling her mom that night. Would she be disappointed? Mad? Concerned?

Stephanie, the student aide, said nothing as she led Brianna down the hallway to the front office. The walk seemed so long. Brianna's sneakers squeaked across the linoleum floor as she made her way past bulletin boards with flyers and announcements, all talking about the Drury Gables Annual Pumpkin Festival in just four short weeks.

Apparently, the festival was the small town's claim to fame. Farmers from all over Pennsylvania came to show off their gorgeous pumpkins and win the grand prize of five thousand dollars and a blue ribbon. Brianna assumed she wouldn't be going. Uncle Shane didn't seem the type to like festivals, and it would be too far to walk by herself.

Still, she could use some festival fun—silly game booths with food stalls full of delicious things like grilled corn and funnel cakes.

As she passed a collage of photos from previous years, Brianna saw something that made her stop dead in her tracks.

It was a photo of a group of kids dressed in autumn colors and holding vegetables that would be found in a cornucopia, all of them smiling for the camera. And it was the smile that threw Brianna off because she would've never imagined that the girl on the far right could smile, or even knew how to. But there was no mistaking the orange dress, the cream-colored ribbon, or her shiny black shoes and short brown hair.

It was the ghost of Shadowrun Road.

But she was alive and happy.

With shaking fingers, Brianna touched the photograph as her gaze jumped down to the caption below it. It seemed to have been taken from an old yearbook.

From left to right: James Smelter, Sandra Hilden, Alex Dorham, and Elisa Maybel, each bringing a vegetable for the fourth-grade class's cornucopia.

Elisa Maybel . . . Was that the ghost's name?

"Hey, Brianna!" Stephanie called, already far ahead at the end of the hall. "Hurry up!"

Brianna jerked her gaze away from the photo. "Coming!"

Swallowing hard, Brianna waited until Stephanie went into the front office before tearing the photograph off the bulletin board and stuffing it into her back pocket. It was concrete proof that this ghost girl had existed, and there was no way she was going to ignore it.

"Brianna." The school's head secretary, Mrs. Brickman, looked up from her ancient computer when Brianna entered the office. "Head on back. They're expecting you."

They?

With lead footsteps, Brianna trudged to the back office door, where she saw an old, tarnished gold plate that read PRINCIPAL HUCKLES. She raised one hand and clenched her teeth when she noticed it was shaking. She wasn't afraid of some principal she'd never see again after this month. She had other things to be scared about. Like ghosts.

She knocked, and the deep voice from beyond the door said, "Come in."

Brianna stepped inside and received her second shock in the past ten minutes: Sitting across from Principal Huckles was Uncle Shane, looking grouchier than she'd ever seen him. That alone made her want to slam the door on them and run all the way back to Texas.

"Um," she began, "did I do something wrong?"

Principal Huckles was about Uncle Shane's age, but he was balding and wore small reading glasses. "Take a seat, Brianna."

Brianna walked around the chair next to Uncle Shane, dropped her backpack on the floor, and took a seat.

Uncle Shane said nothing to her; he just folded his arms and sighed.

As she sat there, waiting to learn what these adults wanted with her, she glanced around at Principal Huckles's office. She'd never been in a principal's office before. There were some plaques and framed awards on the wall, along with an old clock with bronze hands. In the corner to her left was a tall bookshelf, but rather than holding large books, it held mostly personal items like photographs of a much younger Principal Huckles, models of old cars, and other assorted knickknacks.

Principal Huckles laced his fingers and leaned forward on his desk, drawing Brianna's attention. He rested his elbows and looked down at her in that stern principal way. "Kristen told me she overheard you spinning some disturbing tales."

Brianna stared at Principal Huckles. She got called to the principal's office because she'd been talking about the ghost?

"I just wanted to have this talk, with you and your

uncle," Principle Huckles said, nodding at Uncle Shane, "to say that here at Drury Gables School, we don't spread rumors or wild tales that could upset others."

"Rumors?" Brianna repeated. "I wasn't spreading rumors. I was just asking Jacob about the ghost on Shadowrun Road! I see her sometimes when I walk from the bus stop!"

"Now, Brianna," Principal Huckles interrupted in a loud, deep voice, "I don't know what you saw, but you should know at your age that there's no such things as ghosts."

Brianna's face heated up again. She was tempted to argue further, hating the fact that they saw her as a troublemaker, but she knew how this would go. Principal Huckles would calmly insist that what she saw had been a trick of the light or simply her imagination. Uncle Shane would just sit there, annoyed for being called here on account of his troublesome niece.

"Until you get over this little ... fright," Principal Huckles continued, "I think it's best if your uncle drives you to and from school. Don't you agree, Shane?"

"Hhmph" was the only sound that came out of Uncle Shane, his arms folded tightly.

Brianna glanced at Uncle Shane, and predictably, he was scowling deeply. But instead of trying to convince them she wasn't a liar, she folded her arms and pursed her lips.

She knew what she had seen. Even if no one wanted to talk about it, that ghost—Elisa Maybel—was out there, waiting for her, on that road. And Brianna had proof, too. The photo in her back pocket had all but confirmed it, and she was dying to get home and look at it more closely.

7

The whole ride home, Uncle Shane was silent. To be honest, Brianna had been expecting a lecture on how rude it was that she was inconveniencing him. Things like "Don't you have any respect for other people's time?!" and "Don't you understand the value of hard work?!"

But Uncle Shane never said a word. He just frowned at the road ahead and gripped the steering wheel with white knuckles, almost like an explosion was boiling just under the surface.

Finally, he turned up the driveway and parked outside the farmhouse next to a pile of rusty junk. Brianna grabbed the door handle, about to bolt, when Uncle Shane said, "Hold on there a second, kid."

Great, here's the lecture, Brianna thought irritably. *Why did he wait until we got home?*

She was dying to get up to her room to look at the photo of Elisa, but what Uncle Shane said next was the very last thing that Brianna had expected.

"Look, kid, I haven't lived with anyone in a long time, and if you're feeling lonely . . ."

Brianna could barely believe it. He must have thought that he was neglecting her and she was doing this for attention. "I'm not making this up!" she shouted. "I definitely saw a ghost, Uncle Shane. It was a little girl, around nine or ten, wearing an orange dress and—"

"All right, enough." Uncle Shane sighed. "I don't know if you heard other kids talking about her or not, but you should leave this alone, Brianna."

For the first time, Uncle Shane had called her by her name, and his voice wasn't snappy or grouchy, either. It was tired and weary. And maybe even a little sad.

"But she won't leave *me* alone!" Brianna argued.

Uncle Shane's gaze cut to her, suddenly cold and angry. "I have watched kids time and again walk up and down my road searching for this so-called ghost on dares, and I don't want my niece getting roped up into some silly old legend."

Dares? Legend? What was Uncle Shane talking about?

"But—"

"I won't tell your mother about this," Uncle Shane interrupted, "and I'll take you to school as much as my job'll let me, but you're going to have to forget whatever you heard. Those kids at school—they're talking about stuff they don't know. None of them have any respect for the dead," he snapped.

With that, Uncle Shane slid out of the truck, slammed the door, and stomped up on the porch, leaving Brianna in the truck, completely bewildered.

A few things were clear, though: There was a ghost legend in this town, and while some in Drury Gables treated it as a joke, others, like Uncle Shane and maybe even Principal Huckles, didn't like hearing about it at all. But why? What was the story behind the ghost of Shadowrun Road?

Brianna was determined to find out. She grabbed her backpack and hurried out of the truck, into the house, and up the stairs. She shut the bedroom door behind her, took out the photo from her back pocket, and stared hard at the girl in the orange dress.

She looked so different. Full of life and happy, while holding her large pumpkin with a prizewinning blue ribbon on it. But Brianna had seen that orange dress with its cream ribbon sash twice now, and she was sure she'd never forget it. This Elisa Maybel was the ghost on Shadowrun Road.

Hoping for more clues, Brianna turned the photo around and found a date on the back: *October 28, 1994*. Had she died that day? It was possible since she was wearing the same dress, but Brianna couldn't be sure.

Unfortunately, this photo answered only a

number of questions in a much larger mystery. How did Elisa die? And why was her spirit haunting Shadowrun Road? And why did she only appear on Fridays?

"What happened to you, Elisa?" Brianna whispered to Elisa's smiling face.

∽ 🎃 ∼

One . . . two . . . five crows landed on the branches directly above her. They stared down at her with glowing red eyes and hopped from branch to branch, as if eager—hungry—for something.

The crows scared her. She wanted to get up and run away. Run back home. Except she couldn't move. She was so cold. Why had she worn her short-sleeved satin orange dress on such a chilly day? Because it had matched her pumpkin, that's why. But where was her sweater? She was freezing without her sweater. Oh, that's right. She had wrapped it around her prizewinning pumpkin, but that was gone, too. Smashed all across the road. In fact, if she could've moved her hand, she would've felt the gooey innards of the pumpkin against her frigid skin.

Suddenly, a black shadow loomed over her, blocking out the moon and the crows, covering her in a blanket of darkness . . .

Brianna woke up with a gasp, cold and sweaty. She sat up in her bed and shook her hands, as if she could feel the smushy bits of pumpkin on her fingers and palms. Already, the details of the dream were beginning to fade. But she remembered the orange dress and, of course, the pumpkin. It was similar to the dream she'd had at the airport. Like it was another memory but not her own.

Could it have been Elisa's? Was she dreaming about Elisa somehow? Why did she keep having these dreams? More than a little freaked out, Brianna hurried to the bathroom to wash up and get ready for school.

The ride to school with Uncle Shane was awkward to say the least, and by the time he dropped her off, she was actually looking forward to school. His truck peeled away in a billow of exhaust fumes and squeaky brakes just as Brianna's classmates got off the school bus. Out of the corner of her eye, she noticed Jacob watching her, but then she also noticed Kristen, so she hurried into the school building.

Brianna's classes moved at a snail's pace, and by the time lunch and recess came along, she was practically bouncing in her seat with anticipation.

She was barely listening as Mr. Franklin stood at the front of the class and waved around a sheet of paper. "Remember, class, you need to get your permission slip signed by a parent to ride the bus directly from school to the Pumpkin Festival. I need them signed no later than the Monday of the festival week."

Just as he was finishing his announcement, the lunch bell rang, and all the other students hurried out of the classrooms, talking and laughing with their friends. Brianna usually ate lunch from the school cafeteria using the lunch money her mother had given her to last the two months, but she decided to skip lunch today. Even though her stomach would punish her later, she had only one good chance to do a little bit of research.

If going to the library during recess for the past three weeks to sketch had taught her anything, it was the lunch habits of the librarian. Mrs. Reynolds would eat her

Italian leftovers and read a thriller novel that had a cover with big, bold letters and a cityscape in the background, then she would emerge during the second half of the period to help kids check out books.

As quietly as possible, Brianna padded across the carpet and slipped into the old wooden chair in front of the third computer. She knew that one to be the fastest out of the four computers because it was the most popular.

Quickly, Brianna logged in and navigated her cursor to the search engine icon. Bringing up the internet home page, she typed *Elisa Maybel 1994*, but just as she was about to hit enter, a hand shot out and clicked the button on the monitor, killing the power to her computer.

"Hey!" Brianna cried, leaping from her chair and whirling around to find . . .

Jacob Dorham.

Unfortunately, her shout drew Mrs. Reynolds away from her chicken marsala and book. "Brianna? Jacob?" she asked, coming out from the back room. "What's going on?"

"We're fine, Mrs. Reynolds," Jacob said, grabbing Brianna's arm and tugging her toward the library door. "Sorry to interrupt."

Before Mrs. Reynolds could say another word, Jacob was hauling Brianna out into the hallway.

The moment they were clear from the library and from earshot of Mrs. Reynolds, Brianna yanked her arm out of Jacob's grasp.

"What'd you do that for?" she snapped.

"How did you find out her name?" Jacob snapped back. "Who told you? None of us are supposed to talk about it."

"No one told me. I—"

"Shhh!" Jacob pressed a finger to his lips. Then, after looking right and left, he grabbed Brianna's arm again and pulled her into the custodian's closet. Once inside, he turned on the lights and leaned against the doorknob. The one light bulb hanging above their heads bathed them in a gold glow and cast dark shadows into the corners behind the mops and brooms and buckets. Jacob's freckled face looked almost sinister in the bad lighting.

"We're not supposed to talk about Elisa at school. Did Corey tell you? Did he pull a prank?"

"No! Well—yeah, he did, but he didn't tell me her name." Brianna fumbled for the photo in the pocket of her hoodie and shoved it into Jacob's hands. She jabbed her finger at Elisa holding her pumpkin. "I've seen that girl on the road, and I recognized her on the Annual Pumpkin Festival bulletin board—you know, in that collage of photos. The caption said her name is Elisa Maybel. What happened to her?" Brianna said in a rush, her words going so fast they almost blended together.

Jacob stared at the photo for a while, then handed it back to Brianna. With a frown, she took it back. *I guess he won't tell me, either.*

"No one knows."

Brianna stared at Jacob in shock. "What do you mean no one knows?"

"I *mean* she just disappeared one day. The last time anyone saw her, she was walking home from the festival, but she . . . she never made it home. Her parents reported her missing that night and there was a big search for her but all they found—"

Jacob swallowed, his eyes big and fearful.

Goose bumps erupted on Brianna's arms. "What did they find?"

"Just her foot."

"*What?*"

"I know, it's like a horror movie, right?" Jacob shivered. "But that's all the police found on Shadowrun Road. Legend has it that Elisa's ghost haunts the road. She limps down the road searching for her missing foot. And if she can't find her foot . . . then she steals someone else's."

It was as if someone reached into Brianna's chest and gripped her heart with icy fingers, stopping it entirely. A ghost that limps along and steals people's *feet*?

Now it all made sense. The footsteps—the *STOMP, shhh, shhh* sounds.

Brianna's knees went weak, and she stumbled against the shelf full of cleaning supplies. A few rags rained down on her, and she felt Jacob pick them off her as he said, "Brianna? You okay?"

She grabbed Jacob's wrist on the hand that held a rag and she stared at him with wide eyes. "Jacob, I can *hear* the footsteps behind me. Elisa is after me!"

Jacob's face had gone terribly pale. "It's just an old legend."

"But it's real! I saw her with my own eyes! Why doesn't the town warn people?"

"Look, there's a reason we're not allowed to talk about it," Jacob protested. "The older kids used to dare each other to walk up and down the road to see if they could see the ghost. It was like a test of courage for them. It was all fun and games until one kid got hit by a car running across the road. He only had a few broken bones, but that scared the adults bad and now any kid who mentions Elisa gets in trouble."

Well, at least that explained why no one really wanted to talk about the ghost. But Brianna wasn't playing truth or dare; she was just walking home from school!

She needed to know how to survive Shadowrun Road and make it home with her feet still attached to her body. Uncle Shane was driving her now, but he made it clear it couldn't be a permanent solution.

Jacob sighed. "It's why I asked if your mom would be done with her training earlier. Elisa only seems to appear around the anniversary of when she disappeared."

That was a pleasant surprise. Jacob hadn't been treating her like a chore, he'd been worried about her walking along Shadowrun Road during the time frame of the hauntings. She owed him an apology, which she gave. "I'm sorry for ... um, what I said back then."

Jacob shrugged. "It's okay. It came out weird, and I should've tried to explain, but I didn't want to scare you about ... you know ... a ghost."

With a shaky laugh, Brianna shook her head. "I don't think I would've believed you, anyway. It would've sounded like you were trying to scare me to be mean."

"I'm not like Corey," Jacob said, making a face.

Brianna smiled. "I know."

They were quiet for a few seconds before Jacob said, "But your uncle is taking you to school now, right? Maybe you won't have to worry about it."

Brianna could only hope.

∞ 🎃 ∞

The next Friday morning—the first Friday in October—Brianna awoke to a pounding on her bedroom door.

"Get moving, kid. You're taking the bus—today and the rest of the time you're here."

A sharp stab of fear poked Brianna's lungs. "But—"

"I've got a job, Brianna!" he said angrily. "Do you want to call your mom and tell her about this problem we're having?"

Brianna scowled up at the ceiling. That wasn't fair—he knew she wouldn't want to worry her mother. With a groan, Brianna pulled herself out of bed, and as she dressed, she thought through all the ideas of how to avoid Shadowrun Road and its ghost. She could pretend she was sick. But Uncle Shane would never buy it and neither would the school nurse. She could try walking through the woods instead, but what if Elisa haunted the woods, too?

By the time she'd eaten her breakfast and laced up her sneakers, she had run out of ideas. Short of calling her mother and demanding to be taken home—which wasn't going to happen—she had no other options.

Taking a deep breath, Brianna stepped out onto the porch and headed down the long driveway. It had definitely gotten chillier and darker as fall had settled in, but the sunrise was still visible beyond the field of tall grass and through the trees. It was pretty to Brianna in a way that the sunset now wasn't. The sunrise foretold light and warmth of the day, while the sunset cast shadows of darkness and the chill of the night.

Watching her breath come out in clouds, Brianna walked at a breakneck pace along Shadowrun Road, refusing to hear anything, see anything, or notice anything that wasn't three feet in front of her.

It wasn't until she was on the bus that she finally relaxed. Nothing had happened. No ghost. Ignoring the stares of the other kids, Brianna took the seat next to Jacob.

He looked at her with wide eyes. "You're taking the bus."

"Thank you, Captain Obvious," Brianna grumbled. Then she lowered her voice, whispering, "What am I gonna do? I can't walk home and keep both my feet." Brianna thought about the last time Elisa had run her off the road—how the footsteps had been practically on top of her. She shook her head. "Not for the rest of October . . . I'll never make it. Do you think there's some way to make Elisa rest in peace?"

Jacob thought for a minute. "There might be some books about ghosts at the Drury Gables library. We can go tomorrow and check them out."

It seemed as good an idea as any, so Brianna agreed.

The whole day at school, Brianna tried to prepare herself for the walk home. But when the bus dropped her off at her stop, Brianna's hands were shaking. She stuffed them into her hoodie pockets, clenched her fists, hunched her shoulders, and started speed-walking down the road.

The shadows were not only thick, she was swimming in them. Was it just her mind playing tricks on her, or was this road darker than the rest of Drury Gables? There was barely enough light to see her feet, and it felt like she was walking through a black tunnel. Brianna couldn't be sure, but it was as if this lone street was caught in twilight while the rest of the town hadn't yet seen sunset.

The branches knocked against one another as leaves rained down, making creaking and whooshing noises. They were falling faster now. Even the slightest breeze seemed to pull down a whole army of them. Her footsteps crunched and cracked on the dry leaves, and she was tempted to place her hands over her ears—but it was too cold.

That was when a different sound could be heard over the wind, the branches, the leaves, and Brianna's own footsteps.

The fluttering and beating of wings. Crows, at least a dozen of them, swooped down from the branches and came after her. Brianna screamed and threw up her arms, protecting herself from sharp talons and beaks. But the crows didn't touch her—they just showered her with black feathers and screeched in her ears.

Breathless, Brianna ran down the road, her backpack thumping on her shoulders and lower back. What did these crows want from her? They came to her in her nightmares, too. Were they part of the haunting? Did Elisa somehow control them?

Brianna's lungs screamed in agony as she ran as fast as she could. The crows flew up into the trees as another pair of footsteps joined her own. *STOMP, shhh, shhh. STOMP, shhh, shhh.*

Unable to stop herself, Brianna looked back, and she could see Elisa's hunched, lopsided form. Moving faster than what should've been possible, Elisa chased after Brianna, dragging her leg across the asphalt. It left a streak of something dark red that made Brianna's stomach churn.

She kept running. Elisa was coming for her! Could she outrun the ghost?

Just as Uncle Shane's driveway came into view, the road glowed with soft golden light. Brianna twisted around to find two yellow glowing discs in the far distance.

It was a car—just like last time. Would the driver see Elisa? It hadn't last week, but then again, Elisa had shown up in the last second before the driver could've avoided her.

She raised a hand, squinting at the bright light after so much darkness. Beyond the beams, she could make out the type of car. It was an old red convertible, and it was careening toward both Brianna and Elisa.

VROOM.

The headlights grew larger and larger as the car zoomed, much too fast, down Shadowrun Road. It wasn't slowing down. Didn't it see them? Why wasn't it stopping?!

Before it could run her over, Brianna threw

herself off the road into a pile of leaves on the side. As she lay there in the growth, her backside growing cold, she watched Elisa's ghost once again caught in the headlights. The ghost raised her arms in front of her face and let out a bone-chilling scream as the car drove through her ghostly form in a flurry of leaves.

And though it was fast, Brianna got a glimpse inside the car.

It was empty.

No one was driving it.

8

Brianna couldn't keep her discovery to herself for one second longer. The moment Uncle Shane had stepped out to chop some firewood, she called the Dorham residence.

"It was a car!" Brianna practically shouted into the phone the second she heard Jacob on the other end.

"What are you talking about? What car?" Jacob asked.

"I was walking home and saw Elisa again. She was chasing me when a car appeared at the end of the road." Brianna explained without taking a breath. "It ran right through her, Jacob—but no one was driving it!"

"Brianna, slow down—"

"No! Don't you get it? It was a ghost car! I think Elisa was hit by a car! *That's* what happened to her!" Brianna's heart was racing. Not just because of what she'd seen but because she might have uncovered a mystery that *no one* else knew.

"I guess that makes sense... if that's what you really saw."

Brianna squeezed the phone cord, scowling. "Of course I saw it. Don't you believe me?"

Jacob hesitated. "Well..."

"Fine!" Frustrated, Brianna hung up the phone forcefully, then sighed and threw herself into one of the kitchen table chairs. She didn't know why she had bothered. It was why she hadn't wanted to rely on Jacob—or anyone else in Drury Gables—in the first place. They didn't know her, and they didn't *want* to know her. Not like her mother or her friends back home. *They* would know she wasn't lying.

~ ❀ ~

That night, Brianna's dreams were haunted by black shadows, red eyes, and yellow beams stretching across gray roads. It was never just one scene but many, all flashing on top of one another like special effects in a movie. When Brianna woke up the next morning, she remembered what Jacob had told her in the custodian's closet. *"It's like a horror movie."*

Brianna even reached down into her blankets to grab her feet to make sure they were both there.

The next morning after breakfast, Uncle Shane called Brianna outside. She was surprised to find him crouched next to an old bicycle and cleaning it off with a rag.

As Brianna came down the porch steps, Uncle Shane stood and inspected the bike, hands on his hips. "It's old," he started, tucking the rag into his jeans back pocket, "and a little rusty in some places, but I cleaned off the cobwebs and put air in the tires."

Brianna could only stare in shock. When she

realized that Uncle Shane was waiting on her reply, she asked, "Is this for me?"

Uncle Shane gave her a funny look. "Of course it's for you, kid. Last night you mentioned you and the Dorham boy were going to the library. Figured it'd be faster on a bike, so I went out to the barn to see if I had one, and luckily I did."

It had been just passing dinner conversation, but when she had told Uncle Shane about spending the day with a friend, he had asked a surprising number of questions: *Where are you going? How long will you be gone? Who's going with you?*

Brianna answered to the best of her ability, but when she inevitably told him that she'd be spending the day with Jacob Dorham, her uncle had relaxed. Apparently being the mayor's son counted for something even with her uncle, because Uncle Shane had asked no more questions after that and finished his pork and rice.

Truthfully, after her phone call with Jacob last

night, she wasn't sure if she wanted to go to the library with him anymore. If he wasn't going to believe her, why should she bother? But now that her uncle had gone to the trouble of getting out this old bike, she didn't see a polite way to get out of it.

Jacob showed up at Uncle Shane's house just after lunch. He, too, had a bike and was happy to see Brianna had one as well. Uncle Shane stood on the porch, looking almost menacing as he leered down at them.

"Just to the library and back. And you better be home before dinner, kid."

"Sure, Uncle Shane," Brianna called over her shoulder as she and Jacob started off across the gravelly driveway.

∼ 🎃 ∼

Years ago, the Drury Gables Public Library had probably been the most beautiful building in town, but time had faded the once bright red brick and the once shiny wood floors.

As Jacob led Brianna through the old stacks of

books upon books, he kept glancing back at her with a frown.

Finally Brianna stopped and put her hands on her hips. "What is it?"

"I do believe you," Jacob said. "About you seeing a ghost car, I mean."

Brianna raised an eyebrow. "You do?"

Jacob shrugged. "I thought about it more last night, and, well, I was thinking about how freaked out I'd be walking down that road by myself. There's no way I'd make something up like that just for fun. So if you think you saw it, I believe you."

"I *know* I saw it."

Jacob looked down at his sneakers as he scrubbed the tip of his right one against the floor. It made a loud squeak. "I also think you're really brave for going down that road by yourself."

"You do?" Brianna asked again. "Really?"

"Well, yeah." Jacob cleared his throat and began walking again. "The paranormal books are down here."

Brianna glanced around at all the rows of books. "How do you know where everything is?"

"My mom's the mayor, remember? I had to volunteer here a lot."

Jacob stopped at an aisle and bent down to look at the bottom shelf. He pulled out a dusty book that had the words *Ghost Lore and the World Beyond the Veil* scrawled across the cover. He pulled out three more, all with supernatural and ghost titles, then found an empty table and started flipping through the old pages.

Most of the books talked about how to communicate with ghosts and how to conduct séances—these special rituals where you called upon a spirit to talk to them. But Brianna didn't really want to talk to Elisa; she wanted to find out how to make the hauntings stop.

In the second book, Brianna finally found a chapter that seemed helpful. "Many wonder why ghosts exist in the first place," she read aloud. "We find that the spirits cannot fully pass on because they have some unfinished business left behind. For some, it is communicating with a loved one, but others, typically the ones who die a more violent death, are left wanting vengeance. Either way, ghosts are often put to rest when they can find peace in death, whether that happens by leaving a message for their family, bringing their murderer to justice, or perhaps having their remains given a proper burial."

Brianna slammed the book closed, beyond frustrated. "How can Elisa find peace in death when no one could ever find her body?"

Jacob tapped the book with his index finger. "Maybe that's what we have to do! Find Elisa's body."

"But how? We don't even know who was driving that car that hit her."

"But maybe if we find out, that'll help us find her body or at least bring her murderer to justice. What do you remember about the car?"

Brianna thought back to the ghost car and pushed down the shivers that came with it. "It was red and old-looking. Like an antique convertible."

Jacob shook his head. "I don't know of anyone in town with a car like that."

"Well, her death was so long ago, the owner might've sold it by now."

Jacob thumped the table with the side of his fist, as if just remembering something. "Maybe, but we might be able to look into what exactly happened back then. What did you say the date was on the photograph you found?"

"It was October 28, 1994," Brianna answered automatically.

"I've got an idea—come on!"

More than curious, Brianna followed Jacob, who strode confidently to the large oak reception desk. A woman who looked as if she had once lived before the Civil War sat at the desk, knitting. Her hair was pulled back in a tight bun and half-moon glasses sat perched upon her hawklike nose. At Jacob's footsteps, the old woman put aside her yarn and knitting needles and leaned over the desk.

"Well, well, Mr. Dorham," the woman croaked in a voice that sounded as if it wasn't used very often. "What brings you here this afternoon?"

"Hi, Mrs. Gobb," Jacob said politely. "Brianna and I were hoping to do some research on the town's history. Can we look at some old newspapers?"

The librarian, Mrs. Gobb, pinched her pale lips to the side as her gaze shifted to regard Brianna. It felt like Brianna was being x-rayed under her gaze, but she must've passed some kind of inspection, because Mrs. Gobb plucked a key ring out of her desk drawer, then stood.

"You'll need to be done by four, Jacob. Library closes at four thirty sharp, you know," she snipped as Brianna and Jacob followed her quickly down the hall. Mrs. Gobb moved pretty fast for an old woman.

"Yes, ma'am," Jacob answered.

They came to a door at the end of the hall, and Mrs. Gobb inserted a key into the doorknob, then gave it a sharp rattle and the door swung open. She reached into the dark room and flicked on the light switch. The room was full of file cabinets.

"All newspapers are saved in versions of micro-fiche," Mrs. Gobb said, gesturing to the rows of cabinets.

"What's microfiche?" Brianna asked.

"Slides that hold readable documents. It's how we stored files before the internet," Mrs. Gobb snapped, then turned to Jacob. "Do you remember how to use the machine?"

"Yes, ma'am," Jacob said again.

With that, Mrs. Gobb turned on her heel and left the dimly lit dusty room, muttering something about *kids these days.*

Not wasting a second, Jacob hurried to a mini TV screen and dumped his backpack on the floor. "Hurry up," Jacob ordered Brianna as he turned toward the rows of cabinets, "look for October 1994."

There were so many cabinets with drawers dating all the way back to 1936 that it took Brianna and Jacob ten minutes to find the cabinet labeled SEPT–OCT 1994.

With care, Jacob pulled out the box of microfiche, and the two flipped through the slides. Finally, they located the date according to the photograph from the school bulletin board: *October 28*. The article about Elisa was the day after: *October 29*.

Jacob fitted the microfiche slide into the holder below the screen and turned on the monitor. Using the controls, Jacob and Brianna zoomed in on the first article.

Unsurprisingly, the disappearance of a girl in a small town was front-page news. Brianna and Jacob were silent as they each read the article.

At 6:00 P.M. yesterday evening, nine-year-old Elisa Maybel went missing after winning first place at the 15th Annual Pumpkin Festival of Drury Gables. When Elisa did not make it home by 9:00 P.M., her parents, Francine and Daniel Maybel, alerted the authorities, and a search party was conducted throughout the town during the night. All that was found was her prizewinning pumpkin smashed across Shadowrun Road. A reward is being offered to anyone who might have clues as to Elisa's whereabouts.

Strange details from Brianna's walks home were starting to make sense. The smashed pumpkin bits on the road because Elisa's pumpkin had been smashed when she'd been hit. And her dreams, too! She remembered holding a pumpkin with a blue first-place ribbon, while walking home on Shadowrun Road, eager to show her parents her prize—only the dreams weren't *hers* at all. They were Elisa's.

"Huh," Jacob muttered.

The simple sound pulled Brianna away from her thoughts, and she looked to Jacob. "What?"

"It was a Friday," he noted. "She died on a Friday. Maybe that's why you only see Elisa on Fridays."

Brianna nodded her agreement. It would make sense. Hugging her sweatshirt closer, she licked her lips and moved the controls to view the next page. "Is there more?"

"Not on this day," Jacob said, already turning to the box of microfiche.

It took them a half hour to find an article that talked about Elisa Maybel again. It was nearly two whole months later. The date was December 15, 1994, and the article was painfully brief.

The search has continued for Elisa Maybel, who disappeared a little less than two months ago. Police are organizing another search party throughout the woods stretching through where Elisa was last seen. Anyone able to help the search should show up at the town square at 12:00 P.M. this Saturday, December 17.

As Brianna finished reading the last word, two things happened at once. The temperature in the room seemed to drop ten degrees, and the lights above flickered eerily. She tried to ignore the lights and the chill and focus instead on the dusty yellow screen.

The next article was the Sunday paper.

The town-wide search for Elisa Maybel has yielded only one clue for the local police. A disembodied foot that appears to have belonged to a child was found in the woods surrounding Shadowrun Road. The foot was sent off to the forensics team in Philadelphia yesterday. A funeral service for Elisa will be held next weekend at Drury Gables First Methodist Church.

Blinking back tears of horror, Brianna turned back to the files of microfiche. There had to be more. There just had to be.

An entire hour passed before they found the next article. It was all the way in April of the following year, and it was even shorter than the last.

The case of Elisa Maybel's disappearance and supposed death has gone cold. A reward for any leads to the case is still being offered. Contact the Drury Gables Police Department for details.

"That's it? No way!" Brianna cried, reaching for the microfiche box again. Jacob grabbed her wrist. His hand was like ice.

"We don't have time. The library is gonna close soon."

"But we still don't know how to find her body."

"Well, we know they found her foot in the woods. Maybe we could start there." Jacob hugged his arms. It had gotten even colder inside the room—to the point where they could see their breath. "It's freezing in here," Jacob said between chattering teeth.

"It's because *she's* here," Brianna whispered.

Jacob stared at Brianna. *"Who's* here?"

"Elisa." Brianna glanced at the shadowed corner of the room where one light had burned out. It was almost as if she could *see* the outline of a young girl. She wasn't sure how she knew Elisa was here, but she did.

Jacob stood, his freckled face pale. "That's not funny. Stop trying to scare me."

"I'm not," Brianna hissed back. "That's why it got

so cold. It always feels like this on the road when she's around."

"But how can she be here? I thought you said she only showed up on Fridays?"

Brianna thought back to the book they'd just read. "Maybe she knows we're trying to help her with her unfinished business."

"We should get out of here," Jacob said, shoving the slides back into the box out of order. He was so scared, he didn't even care about the wrath of Mrs. Gobb.

But Brianna was tired of being scared and running away. Maybe this was her time to finally face this ghost without worrying about her foot being stolen. "Elisa?"

The lights flickered.

"Bree!" Jacob yelped, springing away from the microfiche machine.

Brianna turned bravely toward the shadows. "Elisa, if we find your body … will you be able to rest in peace?"

The light bulbs suddenly burst. Brianna and Jacob

screamed as sparks flew and a shower of glass rained down on them. They both sprinted out the door and ran down the hall. Their footsteps pounded throughout the empty library, and they nearly knocked over Mrs. Gobb as she got up to check on all the commotion. Even with Mrs. Gobb's yells for them to come back and not to run, Brianna and Jacob didn't stop.

Out in the parking lot, they each grabbed their bikes and pedaled home as fast as they could. The whole time, Brianna couldn't help but think that Elisa had indeed answered her.

She just didn't know if it was yes or no.

9

The rest of the weekend, Brianna stayed indoors except on Sunday, when she and Uncle Shane went to the grocery store. Brianna had picked out a barbecue sauce that Uncle Shane actually seemed eager to try—meaning he'd made more than one grunt when Brianna placed it in their grocery cart. He'd made *two* grunts. Brianna counted that as progress.

While her barbecue chicken was cooking in the oven, Brianna called her mother.

"How was your weekend, sweetie?" Mrs. Jenson asked. She sounded tired, but Brianna knew that was because she'd spent most of the weekend studying for her training program.

"It was good," Brianna said, and it actually didn't feel like a total lie. "I went to the library." Even though the trip to the library had been scary at the end, she finally felt like there might be something she could do about the ghost, when it had seemed all but impossible before.

"Oh? With who?" her mother asked.

"Jacob Dorham."

There was a sigh of relief through the phone. "I'm so glad you found a friend there. You didn't have many friends when we lived up there. Well, except for your imaginary friend," she added with a laugh.

Brianna frowned. "I didn't have an imaginary friend." At least, she didn't remember having an imaginary friend in Drury Gables. She barely remembered anything about this town.

"Sure you did, sweetie, but that was normal for kids your age," her mother continued casually. "Although you stopped talking to her immediately once we moved to

Richland. It was almost like you left her behind in Drury Gables."

Before Brianna could ask anything else about her imaginary friend, Uncle Shane's deep voice boomed from the living room.

"Brianna, you're going to burn the chicken!" Uncle Shane's voice called from the living room. It was only then that Brianna recognized the strong smell coming from the oven. With a quick goodbye to her mother, Brianna hurried to finish the rest of dinner, half her mind wondering who this so-called imaginary friend had been.

She was still trying to remember this friend when she went to bed that night. But a crow's screech outside her window drove out thoughts of friends and brought in thoughts of the dead . . .

∾ ◍ ∾

The week passed by uneventfully—meaning, no hauntings. But as Friday crept closer, Brianna's stomach tied into tighter and tighter knots. She was facing another walk home with Elisa's ghost.

Over the week, Brianna and Jacob had discussed when to search the woods for clues to find Elisa's body. Going right after school was out of the question because Jacob needed to get straight home to help watch his baby sister. It was also why he couldn't walk home together with Brianna. As a result, she was left to face Shadowrun Road alone yet again. By the time the bus dropped her off, Brianna had run through at least five different scenarios of how she might be able to escape Elisa's ghost. None seemed very possible.

With a deep breath, Brianna began to half walk, half jog down the road. The trees were the shade of a smoky gray in the fading light, and the leaves were now all brown—dry and dead, devoid of life and color. The branches looked like crooked witches' fingers, and the October chill bit at Brianna's cheeks and neck like nothing else ever had.

As she moved her hands up and down her arms to generate some warmth, she heard them.

Footsteps.

At first, they were faint, just like before—more like echoes of her own steps. But then they got stronger and louder.

STOMP, shhh, shhh.

Brianna resisted the urge to stop and look back. If she did, would she see Elisa?

STOMP, shhh, shhh.

The cold was paralyzing now. Freezing. It had to be colder than anything that was possible in Pennsylvania. This was like Siberian cold. Or the North Pole cold. Maybe even Pluto cold. It made her fingers hurt and her bones ache. Walking through it felt like walking through sludge.

STOMP, shhh, shhh. STOMP, shhh, shhh.

The steps came at her faster now, and Brianna felt like she was going slower, even though she was *trying* to run. Was it the fear or the cold holding her in place?

STOMP, shhh, shhh. STOMP, shhh, shhh. STOMP, shhh, shhh.

Either way, Brianna knew she couldn't make it all

the way to Uncle Shane's house. Not before Elisa caught up to her. She needed to get away somehow.

STOMP, shhh, shhh. STOMP, shhh, shhh. STOMP, shhh, shhh.

Brianna's gaze jumped to the right and the left. The woods. She didn't like the idea of going into them. After all, that's where Elisa's foot was found, but then ...

VROOM.

Brianna glanced over her shoulder and once again was blinded by the bright yellow headlights. The red paint of the old convertible gleamed like blood, and the silver tire rims flashed as they swerved into view.

Her legs ached and yelled at her, but she commanded them to move faster and faster until she jumped off the shoulder of the road into the bank full of leaves. Her sneakers sank into the dry, cold piles, but air seemed to move through her lungs faster. It wasn't as hard or as painful to move.

Still driven by terror, Brianna clambered up the bank of the woods, darted through an opening in the trees, and kept running. Her strength returned as she crashed through the dense woods, dodging trees and bushes and rocks, the sound of the ghost car's engine fading with each step. Her sneakers slipped and slid on the thick layers of leaves coating the forest floor.

She concentrated on getting the feeling back in her fingers and the sweat beading on her temple and under her arms. It was still chilly outside, but she was also hot from running. The farther she seemed to get from the road, the less . . . *haunted* everything became.

Finally, when she couldn't take another step without collapsing, Brianna slowed down, breathing hard. There was a painful stitch in her side, and the muscles in her legs complained loudly for being pushed to their limit. She took a few more steps before she gave up and hunched over, her hands on her knees, trying to get her panting under control.

The sounds of the woods came back to her. The wind whistled through the forest while the bird calls echoed off in the distance. While it wasn't completely dark yet, the trees and the leaves were thick, casting dark shadows every which way.

She was lost in the woods. Without any idea of how far she was from Uncle Shane's. If she turned right, she *should* get there eventually because it had to be in the same direction, but then she'd woven through a lot of trees, maybe turned in a wrong direction. She wasn't sure. She'd only had the one thought: *Get away from the ghost*.

But being lost in the woods . . . that seemed just as terrifying.

Brianna tried to stay calm as she rotated right and squinted into the gloom of the forest. There wasn't a clear path and the grass was tall. She'd have to pick her way through the growth and around the trees. But if she kept in this direction, she should eventually hit the meadow, where she'd be able to see Uncle Shane's old farmhouse.

Summoning what little courage she had left, Brianna hiked her backpack onto her shoulders and started her trek through the woods.

She had no way of knowing the exact time, but it

was much, much later when she finally lost hope. Through the trees, she had caught the last bit of sun dip below the horizon. Darkness now stretched across the sky like a quilt and the moon was out in a hazy yellow circle, not quite full but pretty close.

Finally, she had to face the cold hard fact: She was lost. If she'd been going the right way, she would've made it back to the farmhouse over an hour ago.

Cold, hungry, tired, and not knowing what else to do, Brianna crouched down, her back resting on a hard tree. Hugging her knees, she tucked her face down under her arms while her shoulders shook with silent, thick sobs.

She couldn't do this anymore. She wanted to be back home with her mom and her friends. Away from the awful kids at school, these woods, Shadowrun Road, and, of course, that ghost.

Every minute here had been worse than the last.

When Brianna took a shuddering gasp through her tears, she heard something over the night wind and her own sobs. Brianna pursed her lips, listening hard, hope rising in her chest.

Because it wasn't footsteps she heard but a soft, gentle humming.

The song was an old nursery rhyme she remembered from when she was really little. The name suddenly came to her: "The Farmer in the Dell."

She looked around, trying hard to see through the gloom of the woods, but couldn't make out even a single figure. While the disembodied humming should have felt creepy, it didn't give her goose bumps or send shivers down her spine. Maybe it was because she'd been so alone and so scared, but she wasn't afraid of the humming.

She stayed still against the tree, listening, as the humming got louder. It got so loud that the person humming would have to be right next to her ear . . . but still, she saw no one.

Then the humming started to fade.

Brianna leaped to her feet, not wanting the humming to go away. She couldn't explain why, exactly, but the nursery song calmed her. If it left, she would be all alone again.

Rubbing her hands together for warmth, Brianna started following the lighthearted tune as best she could. Sometimes it would grow soft, and she would need to pause and listen and then change direction, rewarded by the song being louder whenever she did so.

When the humming finally faded, the break in the trees came into view up ahead. Breathless with relief, Brianna raced through the woods toward the tree line and broke free of the woods, stumbling right into a field of wheat. Off in the distance, illuminated by the moonlight, was a barn.

For a moment, Brianna just stood there, staring at the barn and the surrounding field. A bit away was also a scarecrow and a tractor . . . it all looked so familiar. Then she remembered—she had sketched this exact scene once on Shadowrun Road!

The humming started up again, and when Brianna turned in its direction, she was shocked to find Elisa standing close by, in the middle of the wheat stalks swaying in the breeze. She seemed like an ordinary girl—just like from the photo. Clean, alive, and with both feet, too—although pale and slightly translucent.

The ghost waited a moment and then began walking along the tree line. Terrified but following her gut instinct, Brianna walked behind Elisa. Eventually, the barn faded into the distance and another structure came into view—Uncle Shane's farmhouse! Gold light beamed out from the windows while owls hooted and beetles buzzed.

Elisa stopped at the edge of the gravel driveway. The breeze blew and swayed the branches and grass, but neither her hair nor her dress moved.

Brianna held her breath. Elisa Maybel was closer than she'd ever been. Close enough to reach out and touch her with just a few short steps.

Then Elisa's ghostly form shifted from a little girl to something more like a corpse. Her skin peeled off her cheek and arm, showing red muscle and tissue and clear white bone. She was back to being lopsided with her leg bent at an odd angle, blood oozing onto the gravel. Elisa reached out with both her hands toward Brianna. Her blue lips moved, mouthing what appeared to be *"Help me."*

As Brianna stood frozen in utter terror, Elisa grew darker and darker, as if bathed in layer upon layer of shadow. Then her shadow broke apart into a flock of crows, cawing and screeching into the night sky.

10

Brianna screamed and ducked as the crows soared overhead into the woods. It took a long time before she was able to move again and breathe normally. When her fear had finally resided, she made her way up the driveway and the porch steps, thinking hard.

Why had Elisa led her through the woods? Yes, Elisa had guided her back home, but not without first showing Brianna the barn off in the distance. Brianna had even drawn that same scene once on Shadowrun Road. That couldn't be a coincidence. Was that barn significant somehow?

Just as she was about to enter the house, the head-lights of a truck swung into view of the driveway. The brakes squealed as the truck came to a hard stop right at the bottom of the porch steps. Uncle Shane leaped out, panting, his eyes wide with panic.

"Brianna! Where the devil have you been?" he shouted, stomping up the porch steps.

Brianna opened her mouth and closed it. She had no idea what to say. Finally, she went with the truth. "I . . . I got lost in the woods."

Uncle Shane grabbed her shoulders, and for a moment, Brianna thought he was going to shake her. But instead, he pulled her into a tight embrace.

"You scared the fire outta me! I've been looking for you everywhere."

Brianna was so shocked, she couldn't even hug him back. The embrace was short, anyway—he pulled her back out the next second. "What were you doing in the woods?" His voice immediately changed from concern to anger.

"The ghost was on the road, so I went into the woods to get away from her."

Uncle Shane stared at her for a moment, then rubbed a hand over his forehead wearily. "That old legend again? I told you, it's just a dare from the local kids—"

"Elisa Maybel is *real*, Uncle Shane. And she didn't just disappear one night. She was hit by a car!"

A panicked look flashed across Uncle Shane's face.

"How in the world do you know that?"

Brianna opened her mouth to tell him, but he waved his hand.

"Never mind," he said, tired. "All right, kid, you win. I'll drive you home from now on. I'll just have to make it work at the auto shop."

"Really?" Brianna asked, almost dumbfounded. Uncle Shane had mentioned his work at the auto shop a few times, and he always claimed to be very busy there. Could he afford to take off early every day to pick her up?

"Yes, really. Now let's get inside, it's freezing out here."

Uncle Shane surprised Brianna by heating up a frozen pizza in the oven and letting her choose a movie to watch while they ate. The movie ended up being longer than they thought it was, so it was much later than usual when Brianna called her mom for the evening. Her mother answered on the third ring.

"Bree? It's late. It's almost nine." Already her mother's disapproving tone bled through.

"I know. I'm about to go to bed. But Uncle Shane and I were watching a movie."

"Were you?" Instantly, Mrs. Jenson's tone changed to one of pleasant surprise. "What movie did y'all watch?" The conversation then easily shifted to the movie, in which a board game came to life and wreaked havoc through a town.

They talked about the movie for almost thirty minutes before Brianna finally asked, "So how's training going?"

"Oh, it's fantastic, honey. I'm going to pass this exam with flying colors, and then we'll be home. Just a few more weeks!"

Before, those words would've sounded like a dream come true; now, Brianna felt a twinge of nervous panic.

"That's great, Mom."

"What's wrong, Bree? You don't sound very happy about that. Do you love Drury Gables again? Or is it just that you don't want to lose your new friend, Jacob?" Her mother teased.

"No," Brianna said quickly, her cheeks heating slightly. "I'm ready to come home."

Her mother sighed. "I know you are, and so am I. But all teasing aside, you can stay in touch with Jacob. He's real, not imaginary."

Again with the imaginary friend whom Brianna couldn't remember at all. "Are you sure I had an imaginary friend, Mom?"

"Of course, sweetie. What was her name . . . Oh, shoot, it was something like Melinda. Or Melissa, or . . ."

Brianna's blood ran icy cold in her veins. She took a deep breath and said, "Elisa?"

"That's it! So you *do* remember her." The phone slipped from Brianna's hand and banged against the counter. She could still hear her mother calling, "Bree? Hello? Bree?"

Quickly, with numb fingers, Brianna scooped the phone back up and managed to stumble her way through a hasty good night with her mother. Ignoring Uncle Shane's questioning looks, Brianna sprinted up the stairs to her bedroom.

Her imaginary friend had been a ghost. She had actually known Elisa since she was little. It explained why Elisa's spirit was able to communicate to Brianna through dreams and the strange humming, and that time in the library. All those strange occurrences fell outside the usual haunting that took place every Friday on Shadowrun Road. For whatever reason, Elisa had been haunting not just Shadowrun Road but *Brianna*.

But why? Why was she so special to Elisa?

Brianna tried to tell herself that it didn't matter anymore because Uncle Shane had promised to drive her home from now on. No more walks down Shadowrun Road. That simple fact should've given Brianna some relief, but if Elisa's spirit had somehow chosen Brianna to help her finally find peace in death, then would the ghost really leave Brianna alone so easily?

Not only that . . .

She thought back to Elisa's corpse, all beaten and broken and decaying. She'd been terrifying but also incredibly sad. How could Brianna just leave her like that when she might be able to help her—something that her own town obviously hadn't been able to do.

By the time Brianna had settled into bed, she had decided to continue her search into Elisa's death. After all, she'd already found the clue that she and Jacob needed. The mysterious barn that she'd drawn and that Elisa had led her to that night. It seemed to be the first, and best, place to search.

If she and Jacob didn't find anything tomorrow, then Elisa would have to find someone else to finish her unfinished business.

The next day, a beautiful mid-October Saturday, Jacob left his bike next to Uncle Shane's porch and Brianna and Jacob set off through the fields. They followed the tree line that Brianna had walked with the ghost just the night before.

"So she didn't say anything to you?" Jacob asked for the third time.

"No, I already told you I just heard that song," Brianna said, rolling her eyes.

Jacob frowned. "I barely even remember that song,"

"Then why are you humming it?" Brianna asked, looking over her shoulder at Jacob. He'd been humming the tune for the last couple of minutes.

Jacob's eyes were wide. "I'm not humming."

Brianna gasped, frozen in midstep. "The humming—it's back!"

"I can't hear anything—"

"Shhh!"

The farmer in the dell . . .

The farmer in the dell . . .

147

Hi-ho, the derry-o,

The farmer in the dell.

Eager to get there faster, Brianna broke into a run. The singing got louder over the sound of her pounding feet.

"Hey! Wait!" Jacob tore after her, and together they sprinted as fast as they could across the field. The barn came into view, and eventually a dirt road carved its way through the wheat.

When they finally reached the barn, they were both panting and covered in sweat. Rubbing at her aching side, Brianna inspected the barn door.

There was a large padlock in chains threaded through the handles. It hung a few feet above the ground, gently knocking against the wood every time a strong breeze passed through.

Brianna groaned in frustration, slapping the wood door with her bare palm. She winced as a splinter snagged against her skin.

She was so close! But now she was stopped by a

big rusty lock? Hopefully there was a window or something. Without a word to Jacob, Brianna jogged all the way to the back, and sure enough there was a large triangular opening, big enough for Brianna to get through. The problem was getting up there.

As luck would have it, though, large piles of hay bales were all lined up against the back of the barn, stacked up in an almost pyramid shape. The topmost hay bale was just a foot or two below the loft window.

Immediately, Brianna reached for the stack of hay bales, the humming still loud in her ears. But Jacob grabbed the back of her shirt to stop her.

"What are you doing?" Jacob hissed. "You can't go in there!"

Brianna batted his hand away. "I've got to follow the humming. You can stay out here."

After all, she didn't necessarily need Jacob's help. She'd gotten this far on her own, and he questioned her decisions at every turn. Who knew if he *really* believed her about everything she'd said, anyway?

"But—" Jacob protested weakly as Brianna began to climb.

The hay was prickly and warm under her fingers, and bits of it clung to her jeans and hoodie. At the top, she straightened and looked through the loft window—what she saw was nothing special. Just an old barn loft with a wood floor covered in hay, dirt, and dust.

But the humming was blaring in her ears now.

The farmer in the dell . . .

The farmer in the dell . . .

Hi-ho, the derry-o,

The farmer in the dell.

Elisa's spirit was guiding her for some reason or other. It had to be important.

With a grunt and a big heave, Brianna lifted herself over the windowsill, her sneakers scraping against the peeling red wood as she threw her foot over the ledge. She hit the floor in a flurry of hay and dust. She coughed as she rubbed her knee and elbow, sure there would be bruises there later.

Busy picking herself up and dusting off all the hay, it took her a minute or two to realize that the humming was no longer there.

"Elisa?" Brianna called softly in the loft.

There was no movement. Just dust motes floating in the sunlight streaming through the window.

Maybe the humming had stopped because Brianna was where she needed to be. Taking a deep breath, she inched toward the edge of the loft and looked down below into the barn.

Something large was covered by a black tarp in the barn's left side, while the right side was vacant. On the opposite walls were shelves of all sorts of old things— wrenches, power tools, paint cans, gasoline jugs, oil containers, old tires ... mostly all automobile tools.

Moving around to the left side, Brianna slowly lowered herself down the ladder. She jumped the final two rungs and landed with a soft thud. Was someone using this place to work on cars?

That was when her gaze was drawn to the big

thing covered in a black tarp on the left side of the barn. With shaking hands, Brianna took the final few steps over to the car and lifted the black tarp.

Sleeping underneath the tarp was an old red convertible—the same red convertible she'd seen flying down the road with Elisa's ghost trapped in its headlights.

11

Brianna stumbled backward and hit the ground hard, her heart pounding. She hadn't found Elisa's body, but she'd found the car that had hit her.

Sweat collecting on her temples and under her arms, Brianna took a shaky hand and traced the shiny red paint with her fingertips. Someone had been driving this car down Shadowrun Road, hit Elisa, and then taken her body away to hide the awful accident.

But who?

And did Elisa want her killer brought to justice?

Was this why Elisa had led her here? Was this her unfin-ished business?

"Brianna!" An urgent whisper echoed through the barn. Jacob's voice. "Someone's coming!"

She scrambled to her feet, hay flying up around her heels as she raced to the ladder and began to climb. Metal clanging was muffled through the doors, but it was easy for Brianna to make out the sound of the chains fall-ing to the ground as she reached for the next rung.

Just as she was throwing herself over the edge of the loft, the barn doors opened.

Heart racing in her chest, Brianna pressed her whole body to the floor of the loft and inched forward just enough to peer over the edge.

A man's silhouette stood in the frame of the barn doors, and as he stepped out of the shadows, Brianna gasped, clapping her hand over her mouth just in time.

It was Uncle Shane.

Brianna watched as her uncle strode into the barn, grabbing tools and putting away others, working within the space as if he'd done so a thousand, million times before. She held her breath as Uncle Shane filled up his toolbox, took a look around the barn, and then left, locking it up behind him.

Sick to her stomach, Brianna hauled herself over the window's ledge and climbed down the stack of hay. Jacob was waiting for her at the bottom. His expression made it clear he'd seen who'd come and gone from the barn.

"So what was in there?" Jacob asked, his gaze darting from the barn's window back to Brianna's face.

Brianna couldn't find the words. Her brain was still trying to catch up with what she'd just seen.

Her uncle had the key to this locked barn, and inside this locked barn was the car that hit Elisa Maybel. Was there any other explanation than the obvious, no matter how horrifying?

Now that she thought about it, Uncle Shane had mentioned going to a barn a few times over the weekends. It was where he'd gotten the bike for her. There were other things that pointed to his guilt, too, like his hatred of this local legend, his job working on cars, and the fact that he lived off Shadowrun Road, where Elisa had disappeared. Why hadn't she put all these pieces together sooner?

Unable to admit the truth—that she was living with the man who killed the girl who now haunted her—Brianna shook her head. "Nothing," she lied. "Just... y'know... farming stuff."

∽ 🎃 ∾

As soon as Brianna got back to Uncle Shane's farmhouse, she hurried up to her room, locked the door, and refused to leave.

Several times, Uncle Shane called for her. She lied, saying she was busy with homework.

Eventually, Uncle Shane came up to her room and knocked on the door. "Hey, kid, are you okay? You hungry? We could go get burgers."

Brianna sat on her bed, her knees hugged tight to her chest, Elisa's photograph lying on the quilt at her feet. She glanced at the door and felt nauseated once again.

Something in her gut told her that what she feared couldn't be the truth. Uncle Shane might be a grouch, but he wasn't someone who would hide a little girl's body and get away with such a thing.

And yet, how could she deny what she'd seen with her own eyes? The ghost car and the car in the barn had been the exact same—all the way down to the type of rims on the tires.

"I'm not hungry," Brianna said.

"All right. Let me know if you don't feel well, okay, kid?"

"I will."

Uncle Shane's retreating footsteps told her he'd left. It wasn't that much later when Brianna tried to go to sleep, tired of staying up and thinking the same things over and over again.

But her dreams were troubled . . .

∽ ✤ ∽

Darkness stretched on for what felt like forever. Maybe she was in outer space. Space would be cold like this, but there would be stars, and planets, and big, bright moons. There would be light and beauty, not this cold black emptiness. So where was she?

There was nowhere to go and nothing to do but keep walking. Maybe if she walked far enough she would find some light, or a place she recognized. She might even find her way home at last. She'd been walking for what felt like years and years.

It was just when she thought she'd never be able to take another step when black turned to gray, gray turned to red, red turned to orange and yellow—the colors of autumn. Trees and falling leaves across a stretch of gray concrete.

She was back on Shadowrun Road.

Overjoyed, she clutched her pumpkin tight to her chest and walked faster. Light, tapping steps—skipping almost. She would be home soon. Finally. But soon the golden afternoon faded to a chilly evening and then a freezing black night. Her steps grew slower, while an intense hot pain seared through her leg. She looked down and found that her foot was gone. Before she looked away in horror, she even noticed a hint of milky white bone.

She ran.

STOMP, shhh, shhh. STOMP shhh, shhh. STOMP shhh, shhh.

Then, suddenly, the yellow headlights disappeared and the shadows were gone. She was left with only darkness once again.

She started walking.

～❀～

Brianna woke up on the floor. Somehow, during her terrible nightmare, she must've fallen off her bed. Pressing her hand over her heart, she felt it ram against her chest, over and over, proving that she was indeed alive.

But Elisa Maybel was not.

Gasping, Brianna rubbed her eyes, which were wet with tears, as she crawled back onto her bed. She had never been so scared. Not when disembodied footsteps had been chasing her, not when seeing a ghost for the first time, not in the library with Jacob, not when seeing Elisa's awful corpse—nothing compared to the fear of that nightmare.

She'd run so fast and hard that she'd thought her lungs would burst or her legs would fall off, but she still hadn't been fast enough to outrun a car. What nine-year-old could? Brianna whimpered and covered her ears—she could still hear the pounding of Elisa's footsteps as she ran down the road to escape her oncoming death.

In her dream—as Elisa—she'd experienced what it was like to be her ghost.

At least, that's what it had felt like. Walking endlessly in the darkness, and then walking down Shadowrun Road, and then the red car coming for her, her running as fast as she could . . . It seemed like the same sequence of events as the hauntings every Friday. The light footsteps, then the heavy stomping and shuffling, then the ghost car racing down the road.

What if . . .

What if those footsteps on the road every evening that Brianna heard weren't Elisa chasing after someone? What if, instead, Elisa was still running from that car? If that was right, then it meant Elisa was forced to relive her death every Friday up until the anniversary of her death.

And if she was really reliving her death, then that

meant Elisa wasn't actually trying to steal anyone's foot at all. Maybe all she wanted was to get home. It would explain why Elisa had yet to take Brianna's foot, even though there had been plenty of chances for the ghost to do it. In Brianna's nightmare—as Elisa—she'd only had one thought. One desire. And it had nothing to do with her lost foot. She wanted to get home.

Brianna could relate. She wanted to be back home with her mom, too. She shivered and hugged her covers tighter.

Forced to relive your own death over and over again. It was truly terrible, but what could Brianna do about it? Helping Elisa with her unfinished business might mean confronting her uncle about the car in his barn—about what happened on the night of October 28, 1994.

Could she do that? Was she brave enough?

The other option, of course, was to go to the local police. But what could they do about it? Even if they knew Uncle Shane owned that old red convertible, there was no evidence tying that car to Elisa's death. Brianna had no proof! They'd never believe her story about Elisa and the ghost car.

A crow cawed outside the bedroom window, and Brianna jerked her covers up to her nose. The moon was high in the sky, and its light cast pale silver beams across Brianna's desk covered with comic books. Summoning up superhero-sized courage, Brianna slowly got out of bed, dragging the blanket with her and wrapping it around her shoulders. She took a deep breath, stepped over to the window, and looked out.

Sure enough, Elisa Maybel stood outside in Uncle Shane's driveway, looking straight up at Brianna. Her dress was caked in mud, and all up her arms and legs and into her hair were dead leaves. Elisa's form was lopsided again, still without her foot.

Her blood pumping fast with fear—and deep regret—Brianna closed the curtains on the ghost.

"I'm sorry, Elisa," she whispered into the darkness of her bedroom. "I can't help you."

12

The following days were slow and agonizing. It was Brianna's second-to-last week in Drury Gables, but it was somehow worse than her first. She stayed in her room as much as possible and stopped cooking dinners for herself and her uncle. She simply couldn't face him when she thought of what he'd done. Still, a part of her believed that it couldn't be true. Brianna knew he had a kind heart, underneath it all.

He had started leaving dinner outside her room since she wouldn't come down. He tried asking her what was wrong several times on their silent rides home from school. He even threatened to call other kids' parents if she was being bullied. But Brianna insisted that she was just homesick.

On Thursday evening, Uncle Shane made a detour on their way back home. And it wasn't a small one, either. He drove her all the way to Doylestown— a town a whole twenty minutes away where she was allowed to buy a comic book and an ice cream cone from an ice cream parlor a block over from the Doylestown Bookshop. Brianna could only guess the nice gesture was an attempt to cheer her up from whatever was keeping her locked in her room.

As Brianna took a large lick off her cookie-dough-and-chocolate-strawberry ice cream, Uncle Shane cleared his throat and tapped the table with his knuckles. "All right, kid. What's going on with you?"

Brianna shrugged, trying to hide her frown as she thought of Elisa's poor ghost. "Nothing, I'm just—"

"Homesick, yeah. So you've said. But you're going home in just over a week. Shouldn't you be more excited?"

When Brianna didn't answer, Uncle Shane sighed. "Tell me the truth, kid. Is this about that ghost on the road? About Elisa?"

Brianna stopped licking her ice cream. She no longer felt like having the sweet treat—despite how delicious it was.

"Brianna, I told you, it's just a local legend. She's not going to try to steal your foot."

"And what if it's not just a legend?" The ice cream melted down Brianna's fingers. For the first time since going to the barn, she managed to look Uncle Shane in the eye. "If someone really did hit her with their car and hid her body to get away with it, and now she's trapped as a ghost, what would you do?"

Uncle Shane stared at her for a very long time. He seemed to be giving her words some serious thought. "You're really not letting this go, are ya, kid?"

Brianna shook her head.

He heaved another deep sigh. "Well, I wasn't going to tell you this, because I didn't want to scare you any more than you already were ... but if you really do believe you see Elisa, then there may be a reason for that."

Brianna stayed silent, holding her breath, worried that if she said anything, then Uncle Shane would think better of telling her anything.

"You remember that you and your parents used to live close by, don't you?"

Brianna nodded.

"Well, the house that your mom and dad bought used to be the Maybels' old farmhouse. Elisa had grown up in the very same house that you grew up in."

Brianna's jaw dropped in surprise. She had grown up in the same house Elisa had. That could be their connection! Maybe that's why Elisa had come to Brianna when she was younger, and maybe why Elisa now haunted her dreams. Elisa—her "imaginary friend"—must not have followed Brianna after she left Drury Gables. But now that she was back, Elisa had once again found her and had been trying to communicate this whole time. It had all started with that first dream Brianna had at the airport. The second Brianna had come back to Pennsylvania, Elisa's spirit reached out to her, desperate for help. It made so much sense now.

"Oh," Brianna said quietly, not sure of what else to say to her uncle. This knowledge didn't set Brianna at ease. If anything, it made her feel worse. Without Elisa's body—or any proof that the red car hit Elisa—there was no chance in helping her rest in peace.

"And . . ." Uncle Shane reached into his jacket, and Brianna held her breath in anticipation. What was he about to show her?

To her surprise, he took out a few pieces of paper covered in crayon. Laying them out on the little ice cream parlor table, he waved his hand across the drawings. "I found these when I was going through some old things. They're yours."

"Mine?" Brianna gawked at them, chills skating over her arms. Each drawing was a stick figure of what was clearly a girl in an orange dress with a pumpkin.

Elisa.

"Yes. I used to babysit you once upon a time when you were just a toddler, you know. I overheard you and your mom talking about your imaginary friend, and that's when I remembered that you'd seen Elisa back then. I never put two and two together until now. I thought she was just an imaginary friend, too. But I'm starting to believe you, kid." Uncle Shane fixed her with a piercing stare. "So what is she trying to tell you?"

Cold fear crawled through her stomach and into her chest. Did Uncle Shane want to know what she knew about Elisa's ghost because he didn't want anyone finding out his secret? What if he found out Brianna knew about the barn and the old red car?

Brianna shook her head violently. "I don't know. I haven't seen her," she quickly lied, when the truth was that Elisa came to Brianna almost every night in her dreams.

Uncle Shane sat back and nodded, and nothing else was said as they finished their ice cream.

You picked the wrong girl, Elisa, Brianna thought as they drove back home in silence. *We might've lived in the same house, but that doesn't mean I can help you find what you're looking for.*

∽ 🎃 ∾

That night Brianna went to bed early but lay awake for hours. She simply couldn't sleep, no matter how tired she was. She thought of Elisa's rotting corpse standing outside on the driveway and winced at the occasional cawing of a crow.

Sometime past midnight, Brianna must've drifted off because the next thing she knew she was dreaming that she was standing out on Shadowrun Road, barefoot, in her pajamas, and freezing cold.

∽ 🎃 ∾

The smell of rotting pumpkin hung so thick in the air that Brianna could almost taste it. It seemed to be everywhere and nowhere. She looked down at the road that she'd walked so many times and noticed something strange—and new. On the black tar of the road, there were stark white lines, jagged and thin. If she didn't know any better, Brianna would almost think that they were the lines of fingernails scraping across the road, as if someone was dragged and tried to claw their way to freedom.

Swallowing, Brianna began walking down the road, deeper into the shadows, because that was the way home. Her breath came out in steamy clouds as the cold bit into her skin. She tried slapping her arms and rubbing them to warm herself up, but nothing helped. She might as well have been walking through a pile of snow.

Dead leaves hit her bare arms and legs and they felt sharp—so sharp she wondered if she was bleeding. But she didn't dare look. The darkness was closing in and she needed to concentrate on the steps ahead of her.

Tap. Tap. Tap.

The sound came behind her, and Brianna pressed her hand tight over her mouth to keep from screaming. Elisa was behind her again, walking down the road, coming for her.

No, Brianna had to remind herself that Elisa wasn't chasing her but running from her own deadly fate. Still, that didn't stop the inky black fear from seeping into Brianna's chest and taking hold.

Tap. Tap. Tap.

The wind howled and shook the dying branches. They knocked against one another and caused a rattling that echoed through the tunnel of trees. Brianna kept walking farther down the road.

Then a new sound came from behind her. It was a moan. A deep, agonized moan.

Brianna was crying now. Icy tears streaming down her cheeks. She'd never felt fear or suffering like this. Still, she wouldn't look behind her, too afraid of what she'd see.

Another moan echoed in the tunnel, and that's when Brianna felt something sticky and wet at the bottom of her feet. She was walking through liquid of some sort. Unable to stop herself, Brianna looked down at her own feet and found them in a puddle of—

Blood.

Dark red blood. And it wasn't just a puddle. It was a whole river of blood, covering Shadowrun Road like a fresh coat of paint.

It was the color and shine of the red car that haunted the road alongside Elisa's spirit. The footsteps continued across the pavement, across the blood—but now the sound was a little different.

Tap. Squish. Tap. Squish. Tap. Squish.

Brianna couldn't bear it a moment longer, she whirled around, and what she found would stay with her forever.

It was Elisa's foot—only her foot.

Brianna woke up screaming. She tore the tangled blankets off, and they passed right through the shadowy figure at the end of her bed.

Panting from her racing heart, Brianna stared back at the pale, lopsided corpse of Elisa Maybel. Beyond the blue lips and scuffed-up, peeling skin, the ghost's expression was blank. But Brianna could feel the anger and hostility coming from Elisa's spirit. It was layered with torment and suffering and desperation.

From down the hall came the sound of Uncle Shane's door rattling open and his heavy footsteps racing across the carpet toward her room. Elisa's cold, dead gaze snapped to the door, then back to Brianna. Just before Uncle Shane burst through her bedroom door, Elisa merged back into the shadows, where, it seemed, she could never leave.

13

"Let me get this straight," Jacob said as he attempted to toss another soccer ball into a bin. The ball bounced off the corner of the bin, and Brianna caught it.

It was just after gym class, and Brianna and Jacob had been chosen to put the equipment back into the storage closet. They had been awarded this chore because they'd talked all through practice, and Coach Kendrick had said if they wanted to talk so badly, then they could talk while cleaning up.

Neither of them had been very upset about it. If anything, it gave Brianna a chance to finish telling Jacob about her dream and about seeing Elisa at the end of her bed last night.

"You think that Elisa is trapped in some kind of loop, where she's forced to relive her death over and over again. But now she's haunting you because you grew up in her old house and she wants your help to rest in peace."

Brianna stooped down, picked up another ball, and chucked it into the bin. It went in with a bang. "It's the only thing that makes sense. Because up till now, all Elisa's hauntings have happened only on Shadowrun Road, right?" Brianna asked, trying not to get irritated.

Jacob nodded. "That's true. No one has seen Elisa off Shadowrun Road like you have. But you also said she's getting angrier."

"Well, wouldn't you be if *you'd* been forced to relive your death for decades?" Brianna argued.

"Of *course* I'd be angry, but I still don't know what we can *do* about it. No one will believe us!"

He was right. It was the thing that Brianna

had been wrestling with this whole time. No one would believe her. No body. No crime.

Jacob believed her, though. In fact, he'd been the one person throughout all of this who had believed her from the start. But she hadn't been completely honest with him.

"Jacob..." she said with a sigh. "I need to tell you something...else."

"What?" He bent down to pick up another ball.

"I lied when I said there was nothing in my uncle's barn that day. The old red car from Shadowrun Road—the one that chases down Elisa every Friday night. It was there."

Jacob stared at her with wide eyes, the ball in his hands, forgotten. "Then that means your uncle..."

Brianna shook her head. "I don't want to believe it, but no matter how I look at it...if that's *his* barn, then that's *his* car, and if it's his car—"

"Maybe he bought it," Jacob offered.

"He bought it?" A shining ray of hope came

with Jacob's words. This whole time she'd assumed the worst, but maybe there was another explanation out there. "Yeah, maybe he bought it off someone after the accident and had no idea what happened to Elisa that night."

"Look..." Jacob closed the storage bin with all the balls and crossed to the closet door, which was cracked. "Why don't we go back to the barn and see what more we can find? Maybe Elisa still has more to tell you. Maybe she knows where her body is buried and we just have to get her to communicate with us."

"That's a good idea," Brianna admitted. "It's Friday, so Elisa is going to be haunting Shadowrun Road tonight. If I try to talk to her, I wonder if she'll be able to tell me—"

Suddenly, the door was ripped open and Kristen stood on the threshold, her silhouette backlit against the afternoon sun. A gleeful smile spread across her face. "You two are in *so* much trouble."

❦

Fifteen minutes later, Brianna and Jacob were called to Principal Huckles's office. Brianna thought Jacob might be mad at her for getting him in trouble, but he didn't seem very upset by it. In fact, the only thing he said on the way to the front office was "I just hope they don't call my mom."

As it turned out, no parents were called. The front office was bustling with PTA members talking about details for the upcoming Annual Pumpkin Festival. Because the festival happened on a Friday, there would be only a half day of school and the kids would be taken to the festival directly by bus, just like a field trip.

Brianna and Jacob listened for ten minutes to one woman arguing with Mrs. Brickman about who was in charge of the banana bread in the baked goods committee before Principal Huckles finally welcomed them in with a pleasant smile.

"So," the principal said, lacing his fingers together as he rested both hands on top of his big oak desk, "Kristen said she overheard you two discussing a certain incident that occurred on Shadowrun Road."

Brianna and Jacob just glanced at each other, wisely not confirming or denying the story.

Principal Huckles adjusted his glasses with pudgy fingers, his pleasant smile turning into a frown. "Now, Brianna, I'm disappointed in you. We've already gone over how it isn't wise to spread such rumors. I've also been told your uncle is driving you home from school now. There should be no more wild tales about ghosts, correct?"

Brianna pursed her lips and resisted the urge to roll her eyes.

"Brianna?"

She sighed. "Yessir."

"And, Jacob." Principal Huckles shifted his bulk in the chair and turned slightly toward Jacob. "I'm sure your mother wouldn't want to hear her son is engaging in such disrespectful, horrid behavior, like trying to scare others."

Disrespectful? Horrid? Brianna sat up in her chair, now angry. Years and years of being trapped in the same recurring nightmare and unable to rest in peace? Now *that* was horrid.

Brianna couldn't stay silent. "The only thing that's horrid—"

"Bree—" Jacob interjected.

"—is that this town has never found out what really happened to her!"

Principal Huckles suddenly launched himself out of his chair, slamming his palms on the desk. "Ghosts do NOT exist!"

Shocked, Brianna and Jacob leaned back at their principal's shout and away from the flying spittle.

"Ahem." Principal Huckles blinked behind his glasses and took a long, deep breath as he straightened his tie. "You two stay where you are. I'm going to make a call. See if we can't put two children who are so bored that they make up ghost stories to work!"

Without another word, Principal Huckles slipped out from behind his desk and headed out of his office, leaving Jacob and Brianna alone.

With a groan, Jacob slid down his seat. "Great. Now we're really in for it."

"I am *not* disrespectful," Brianna snapped. She stood up and started pacing around the small office, irritated and anxious.

"He's the principal, Bree," Jacob pointed out.

It was just then—as she paced around the office for the third time—that Brianna caught sight of a framed photograph on the bookshelf. It wasn't the gilded gold frame that caught her eye but the subjects of the photo.

"Keep a lookout," Brianna hissed at Jacob as she grabbed her chair and dragged it toward the tall bookshelf.

Jacob jumped to his feet, staring at Brianna. "What are you *doing*?"

"Just let me know when he comes back, okay?"

Grumbling to himself, Jacob turned to watch the hall through the door's window blinds.

Brianna climbed atop the chair and swiped the photo in the gold frame from the shelf. Eager to make sure what she saw was indeed correct, Brianna remained on the chair as she stared at the photo.

A flurry of chills raced up and down her spine.

"Bree. *Psst*. Brianna—he's on his way back. Get down! Hurry!"

Before she could think about the consequences, Brianna was snapping off the back of the frame and slipping out the photo. She shoved it in the back pocket of her jeans and hopped down from her chair just as the doorknob turned. When Principal Huckles walked back into his office, both Brianna and Jacob were in their seats as if nothing had happened.

The principal walked around his desk and said, "Well, I just spoke to the head of the Annual Pumpkin Festival committee, and it turns out she'd love some extra help next Friday setting up the chairs for the award ceremony. I volunteered the both of you to help. So instead of riding over on the bus to the festival grounds with the rest of your class, you will need your parent—or guardian—to bring you early to help set up."

"Yessir," Jacob said.

Brianna just nodded. She didn't trust herself to speak.

"Off with the both of you, then." Principal Huckles waved his hand in a shooing motion and Jacob and Brianna shot out of their chairs, hurrying out of the office as if Elisa herself was right behind them.

When they were finally clear of the main office, Jacob grabbed Brianna's arm, slowing them both down in the hallway from their near run. "What did you take?"

With shaking hands, Brianna pulled out the photo from her back pocket. It was an old photo of two young men—clearly past high school age—standing in front of what looked like an auto mechanic shop, complete with an open garage and cars everywhere. One man was obviously Principal Huckles with his round face, glasses, and larger frame, but the other was also familiar. He was slim, average height, with dark brown hair, and he wore a red plaid shirt. He looked like a much younger version of—

"Is that . . . your uncle?" Jacob asked.

Brianna nodded, swallowing hard, because it wasn't the old photo of her uncle that had her speechless. It was the car that the two men were leaning against.

An old red convertible.

14

"How was school, kid?" Uncle Shane asked Brianna as she got into his truck from the school's pickup line.

"I got sent to the principal again," she admitted.

Uncle Shane heaved a deep sigh. "What happened this time?" he asked as he pulled his truck onto the highway, headed for home.

"Well…" Brianna started, watching her uncle carefully. Last night, she'd been so sure that Uncle Shane was the one who had killed Elisa. She'd even been scared to admit she knew too much in fear of what might happen. But Jacob had given her hope. There could be another explanation, and she needed to be brave enough to look for it.

"Well, what?" Uncle Shane pushed.

Brianna took a deep breath. "Same thing as last time. I was talking to Jacob about Elisa."

Uncle Shane tapped his fingers on the steering wheel. "I thought you said you hadn't seen her anymore."

"It was my nightmare last night. She was in it."

For a long time, Uncle Shane was silent. He just drove on past the cornfields, growing darker with every inch the sun set. "You know... something always sat wrong with me about that poor girl's disappearance. I've always wanted to know what happened to her."

Brianna squinted at her uncle. He *sounded* genuine, but something was... off. She thought back to the stolen photo from Principal Huckles's office with the car that had hit Elisa and killed her. She'd stared at the picture for the better part of the final period, and she could very clearly see the resemblance of Uncle Shane's younger self.

"Uncle Shane, did you know Principal Huckles when you were younger?"

"Of course. We grew up together," he said with a half shrug. "Why do you ask?"

Brianna chose her next words very carefully. "I saw a photo up in his office ... with you and him in front of an auto repair shop. You were both leaning against this old red car."

"Oh yeah." Uncle Shane snapped his fingers. "I remember that day. Drew—er, that's Principal Huckles's first name—he used to work at the shop with me. We both fell in love with this old red Chevy convertible from the sixties. We worked together to restore it, and we fought about who would end up with it once it was finally all fixed up."

"What happened to it?"

"That's the weird thing. One day Drew just decided to ... give it up. Gave it to me and quit the shop right after that. I remember thinking it was pretty odd, but I wanted the car so I didn't put up much of a fight," Uncle Shane finished with a small chuckle.

"Where is it now?" Brianna asked, though she already knew the answer.

"I keep it in a barn off my property. Only comes out when I take it to old car shows. Why? Do you want to see it?" He almost seemed excited to show the car off.

If Elisa's body was still buried at the barn, like she and Jacob had suspected, would Uncle Shane really want Brianna going over there?

"No, that's okay," Brianna said, her mind beginning to race with possibilities.

But she did know one thing for sure: Like Jacob had said in the gym storage room, Elisa had more to tell her.

❧ 🎃 ❧

Before supper, right when the sun was going down, Brianna summoned up her courage and put on her jacket. With a quick word to Uncle Shane that she wanted to take a walk around the house, she hurried out the door, down the porch steps, and over the gravel driveway to the edge of Shadowrun Road. There she stood, facing the tunnel of trees where leaves, spirits, and tragedies dwelled.

You can do this, Brianna told herself. *She's just a scared little girl. Like you.*

But she's also an angry ghost, which is not like you at all.

Brianna considered turning back. As scary as her nightmares had gotten lately, and as creepy as it was to have ghosts and crows outside her window, Elisa hadn't really tried to hurt Brianna or steal her foot. If anything, the dreams and her disturbing appearances had been cries for attention. A desperate way to communicate. But what if the hauntings got worse? What if Elisa got angry that Brianna was ignoring her and dragged her out to the road, where Brianna would share the same fate? Brianna's imagination ran wild with different ways the ghost could come after her.

Plus, there were too many unanswered questions. She'd always wonder if her uncle was really the one who killed Elisa or if it was someone else out there, living freely and unpunished. Brianna *needed* to know the truth now.

It's now or never, she thought. *It's only getting darker.*

Trying not to shiver with every step, Brianna started down the road, this time toward the bus stop. Every step felt like it might be her last as she walked deeper into the cavern of trees.

She'd barely been walking for two minutes before she felt the cold creep up around her ankles and grab hold of her shins. Her muscles ached with the chill, and her bones seemed to freeze. She remembered her nightmare, where the road ran red with blood.

Her breath came out in clouds of steam, and shiver after shiver seized her whole body.

Then the footsteps started. But this time, they were in front of her, not behind.

STOMP, shhh, shhh. STOMP, shhh, shhh.

"Tell me where to find you, Elisa!" Brianna shouted into the cold, dark air.

For a moment, everything was quiet. Silent. Then the wind picked up, blowing Brianna's hair against her cheeks and tossing the leaves into the air. Her clothes batted against her as the branches shuddered and shook overhead.

Brianna whimpered and crouched down as the cold wind blew through her. And yet, almost as soon as it had started, it stopped. The wind died down to nothing more than a breeze, and a few leaves danced around her feet.

Gulping down shallow breaths, Brianna raised her head to find the ghost of Shadowrun Road standing before her.

Unfortunately it was the corpse of Elisa, not the happy, smiling little girl from the yearbook photo.

Her eyes were dark and soulless, while her face was as pale as snow. The skin on her cheek was peeling and decaying, and her lips were icy blue. The orange dress with the satin ribbon was covered in dirt and leaves, and her dark curls hung in messy clumps. Tire tread marks decorated the hem of her skirt, and in her fist was a bright blue ribbon. One leg was normal—ending in a shiny black patent leather shoe. But the right leg ended in a tattered stocking drenched in blood.

It was like seeing the ghost for the first time again—no matter how many times she saw Elisa, Brianna couldn't get used to it. Her terrible eyes, and the evidence of her death all over her skin and dress. Brianna was too scared to move, too scared to say anything at all.

Elisa took a step toward Brianna. *STOMP, shhh, shhh.*

Her movement was just as horrible to watch as it was to hear. Elisa limped, her good foot clamping down on the pavement while her bad leg dragged behind her. Her curls bounced around her shoulders, and her dark eyes seemed to suck in Brianna's very soul.

Brianna recoiled, grabbing her shoulders as if to protect herself. She couldn't run—she couldn't even move. She was too terrified.

STOMP, shhh, shhh. STOMP, shhh, shhh. STOMP, shhh, shhh.

"I'll help you!" Brianna cried, not knowing what else to do, tucking her chin to her chest and squeezing her eyes shut. "I'm trying to help you!"

STOMP.

Opening one eye, Brianna sneaked a peak at the ghost.

Elisa had frozen in her movement, staring at Brianna. Her expression morphing from hollow nothingness to something resembling despair.

Slowly, Brianna stood to face Elisa. "I ... I have something to show you."

Elisa tilted her head. Her bones creaked and rattled at the movement. The sound made Brianna's skin crawl.

Gaze still locked on the ghost, Brianna reached around and took out the stolen photo from her back pocket.

Elisa stared at the photo, then moved a dirty hand to point at the red car in the middle.

"Yes," Brianna breathed, "that's the car. But, Elisa, I can't help you unless I know where to find your body."

As Elisa continued to point at the photo, Brianna looked closer at her fingernails. They were scraped and bloody. *As if she'd scratched the road.* It was like in Brianna's dream. Slowly, Elisa's finger moved from the car to the auto shop in the background. She jabbed her finger at the photo so hard she almost poked through it.

"The auto shop?" Brianna breathed. "Are you ... there?"

Elisa didn't answer. Instead, she lowered her hand, then looked over her shoulder and vanished.

Brianna gasped, turning around in the middle of the road. Elisa was nowhere to be seen. The road, apart from numerous shadows and leaves, was empty.

Suddenly, a sound echoed through the tunnel— the distinct sound of a car engine revving. It was the roar of a monster.

VROOM. Two gold discs appeared at the end of the road.

Overhead, the branches trembled and shook from the vibrations of the ghostly engine.

Brianna turned and ran as fast as she could, the car coming after her like a hungry beast.

Something squished under her feet, and as Brianna glanced down, she slid through the orange mush and her ankle twisted beneath her. She fell to the ground hard, catching herself with her palms and scratching them against the asphalt. Bits of smashed pumpkin lay spread across the road, with large smears of the goo covering the concrete in thick patches.

Brianna tried to get up, but the moment she put pressure on her ankle, pain jolted through her body.

The leaves blew and the wind howled, and the car zoomed toward her. The headlight beams illuminated the road and chased away the shadows to reveal something far more sinister than the dark unknown.

Elisa stood over Brianna, bright and translucent

in the golden glow of the headlights. She looked at the oncoming car, her face twisted with terror.

The car was just seconds away—Brianna couldn't escape. She couldn't run. Everything was coming on too fast.

The headlights came upon her, glowing as bright as the sun. Just when Brianna thought this would be her last moment alive, Elisa reached down and shoved her.

Brianna rolled to the shoulder of the road and looked up just in time to see the red car fly into Elisa— her ghostly form vanishing as the car raced by in a blur of red. The scent of rotten pumpkin, stale gasoline, and metallic blood filled the air.

The whirling leaves settled on the empty road.

Breathing hard, Brianna picked herself up and tested her ankle. It hurt a little, but she could walk on it. Maybe the twist hadn't been as bad as it seemed.

Before heading back to Uncle Shane's farmhouse, Brianna walked out into the road once more and stooped down to pick up the remnants of her photograph. It had been torn to shreds, but Elisa had answered Brianna's question without a doubt.

All that was left of the photo was the piece with the building's sign that said DRURY GABLES AUTO SHOP. The place where Uncle Shane worked.

15

Brianna was struck down by a terrible cold. For two whole days following her run-in with Elisa, she felt achy and feverish and had gone through five boxes of tissues. She could barely get out of bed, much less go to the auto shop and look for places where a little girl could've been secretly buried. Surprisingly, though, Uncle Shane was a good nurse. He fixed her chicken noodle soup and constantly refreshed the wet cloth on her forehead with a cooler one when it got too hot.

On Tuesday, she was good as new and could go back to school. Unfortunately, she'd missed her chance to go to the auto shop during the weekend and would somehow have to find out how to get there before Friday.

Because Friday was the last day of Elisa's haunting of Shadowrun Road. She'd disappear to return next autumn when the leaves would once again cover the road and the biting wind would howl through the tunnel of trees. Except that Brianna wouldn't be there to help her.

Friday was also the Annual Pumpkin Festival, and the entire town was consumed with its preparations. Brianna had never seen so many people out and about in Drury Gables. Trucks lugging big equipment drove to and from the vacant field where the festival would be held. The grocery stores and local craft stores were bustling with vendors stocking up in preparation to sell their food and crafts at the festival.

The school itself seemed to be the center of festival coordination. PE class was held outside in the cold because the gym was used to work on the painting of signs and building of stalls. Wood and paint and large rolls of craft paper lined the walls while members of the Parent-

Teacher Association ducked in and out, their arms full.

As the son of the mayor and the teachers' favorite errand boy, Jacob was constantly being asked to help with various tasks. He was sometimes called out of class several times to do something or other.

Even Uncle Shane seemed to be busy due to the festival. All the farming equipment to be used for tractor rides and corn mazes had to be in tip-top shape.

So by the time Thursday rolled around, Brianna was consumed with worry. In fact, it wasn't until Uncle Shane asked her if she was excited to see her mother on Saturday that Brianna even remembered that she was actually going home in two days.

Which was why, when her mother called that evening, the conversation started with very exciting news.

"I've got a job offer!"

Brianna forced a smile. "That's great, Mom."

"I'm discussing some details with the new company, but it looks like we won't have to leave Richland after all. These two months were worth it, Bree."

Outside the window, Brianna could've sworn she heard a crow cawing, and her gut twisted. "I'm really proud of you."

"Are you all right, honey? You sound a little...sad."

Brianna rubbed at her eyes and struggled to stop her voice from shaking. All this time she hadn't wanted her mother to worry, but she only had two days left. Besides, her mother was so happy. How could she bring her down now?

"Brianna? Talk to me, sweetheart."

Brianna struggled for words, then finally settled on something close to the truth. "I have...a new friend up here. And she has a problem. I've tried to help her, but I think I've failed."

"Hmmm." Her mother's voice buzzed over the receiver, and she was quiet for a minute. "Well, have you tried to help her all on your own? Maybe it's not a one-person job."

"What do you mean?" Brianna asked.

Her mother laughed softly. "Oh, Bree, you've

always been so independent. I'm saying that if she's asking you for help, why can't you ask for help, too?"

Brianna considered this and nodded. "Mom, I've gotta go. I need to call Jacob."

Feeling silly, Brianna rushed to the fridge where she kept Jacob's number pinned up with a magnet. This whole time, she'd relied on him without realizing it. Ever since they'd gone to the library together—ever since he'd *believed* her—Jacob was the one person she'd been able to talk to about Elisa, long before Uncle Shane. But if she was being honest, she'd only been letting him help halfway by giving him half-truths and letting him tag along when she couldn't exactly stomach going alone. Maybe it had been her pride, or maybe since coming to Drury Gables she'd thought of herself as completely on her own, but she could rely on him. They were friends now.

She dialed his number and waited, thinking about what she'd say. They both had their punishment from Principal Huckles tomorrow. They were supposed to go to the Annual Pumpkin Festival and set up chairs, but maybe they could find a way to sneak off . . .

Finally, Mrs. Dorham answered the phone.

"Mrs. Dorham? It's Brianna. Is Jacob there?"

"Oh, hello, Brianna! Sure, one second."

A minute later, it was Jacob. "Hey, what's up?"

"Jacob, we *have* to get that auto shop tomorrow. I know she's there. Do you think we could get there during the festival without anyone noticing we're gone?"

Jacob was silent for a few moments, obviously thinking. "I think I have an idea. Make sure you bring your bike to the festival tomorrow."

∽ 🎃 ∽

It took some convincing, but eventually Uncle Shane agreed to bring the bike in the bed of his truck. Several times he asked why she wanted the bike at the festival, and Brianna lied that some of her friends wanted to ride from the fairgrounds to the school, where they could play soccer.

The entire way to the festival, Brianna was nervous. It was the last day of Elisa's haunting, and even in broad daylight, Shadowrun Road looked dark and sinister. But Uncle Shane seemed to be in good spirits today, and the whole ride there he entertained Brianna with stories of previous years' festivals. Dunking booths, hay rides, caramel apples—the Drury Gables Annual Pumpkin Festival had it all. It sounded so fun that Brianna had almost forgotten that by going to look for Elisa, she'd miss most of it.

As Uncle Shane talked, Brianna couldn't help but think about what she'd find at the auto shop. If Elisa's body *was* there, would Uncle Shane be blamed? Or maybe it really had been him after all—but she just couldn't picture the man who'd taken her to get ice cream and nursed her back to health was the same coldhearted person who'd do such a terrible thing.

Either way, she'd find Elisa's body and then the rest was up to the police. Hopefully finding her body and proving to the entire town of Drury Gables that Elisa hadn't just "disappeared" was what Elisa needed to finally rest in peace.

It turned out that the festival wasn't very far at all from Shadowrun Road. In fact, it was just a mile down the main highway. Brianna was fairly sure that if she cut through the field and the trees, she'd be able to get back to Uncle Shane's house in no time. Since Elisa had lived off Shadowrun Road, too, at Brianna's old home, then it made sense why Elisa thought she could've walked home.

Trucks and big vans and SUVs were parked off the road in the festival field, with what looked like half the town setting up booths, equipment, produce, and food stalls. Not far from where Uncle Shane parked his truck, Brianna caught sight of Jacob standing next to a red-haired woman who was likely his mom, the mayor. Brianna waved at him and he jogged over.

"Where's your bike?" Brianna asked.

"I've been here awhile. It's in the back where we're supposed to set up chairs. C'mon, follow me."

With a goodbye to her uncle, Brianna took her bike and followed Jacob through farmers unloading their pumpkins, volunteers stringing up autumn-themed decorations, all the way to the back, where a small stage had been set up for the award ceremony for the winners of the pumpkin contest.

A fussy woman wearing a badge that basically said *I'm in charge* directed Brianna and Jacob to a stack of chairs. "I want ten rows with ten chairs on each side, and an aisle down the middle. Got it?"

Brianna and Jacob nodded, and the woman went off to bark orders at someone else.

The two kids got to work and as Brianna started on her first row of chairs, she noticed Principal Huckles nearby talking to the fussy woman with the badge— probably about the arrival of the school buses to the festival grounds. Once the festival was set up, the buses would arrive with all the students, who were then allowed to go off and play games and eat treats. It was during that distraction—of the other kids arriving—that Brianna and Jacob would slip away.

Once they finished setting up the chairs, Brianna

and Jacob went around behind the stage and waited for the buses. At the sound of squealing brakes and raised voices, they grabbed their bikes and started off across the fields into the nearby woods.

"Do you think anyone saw us?" Brianna asked as they made it into the shade of the trees.

Jacob looked out at the swarms of children racing off the bus toward the stalls of food and games, and shook his head. "Nah, we're fine."

"Can we really make it to the auto shop on our bikes?" Brianna asked, frowning at the bunch of under-growth in the surrounding forest. It would be hard to ride through, that was for sure.

But Jacob was already leading his bike to the right. "This way!"

Two minutes later, they came upon a well-trod dirt path. "It's an old bike trail that leads into the town square. We can make it there in ten minutes."

Brianna grinned and nudged him with her elbow. "I knew you'd come in handy."

Jacob rolled his eyes and mounted his bike, fighting back a smile. "Thanks, I think."

Biking down the trail did indeed take ten minutes, give or take one or two. And it was a lovely little journey. They followed a stream with water and pebbles that sparkled in the sunlight that shone through the trees. If it hadn't been for the possible dead body at their destination, Brianna would've enjoyed the ride.

The trail opened up to the town square, and Brianna followed Jacob down the main road, and just as they were turning off the side road, that's when Brianna heard it—the humming.

She almost fell off her bike as it came back, loud and clear.

The farmer in the dell . . .

The farmer in the dell . . .

"Jacob!" she called. "It's back! The humming is back!"

Hi-ho, the derry-o,

The farmer in the dell.

The Drury Gables Auto Shop hadn't changed much from the picture. It was a large aluminum building with an open garage and several—albeit newer—cars parked, awaiting their turn to be repaired. The old blue sign was the same, too. All that was missing was the red convertible, and Brianna already knew where that was.

Brianna dropped her bike in the middle of the lot and raced around to the back of the shop, Jacob right on her heels. The humming was pulling her like a physical arm. It resounded in her brain and pulsed through her blood. And she felt cold.

Yes, cold, like ice was running through her veins. It made her fingers numb.

The back of the shop was where all the older parts were taken out, ready for the dump or the junkyard. All around were stacks of old, deflated tires and rusted parts in boxes that had been taken from cars and replaced with new.

The farmer in the dell . . .

The farmer in the dell . . .

Elisa shouldn't be here—not surrounded by this old and rusted junk. She deserved to be buried in a place where her family could visit her and leave flowers by her gravestone.

Hi-ho the derry-o . . .

Finding the place where the humming was the loudest, Brianna dropped to her knees at the corner of the auto shop's back wall and clawed at the dirt. Brianna could feel Elisa's spirit and its desperation running through her like it was her own.

She'd barely made a dent in the dirt when Jacob suddenly grabbed her by the shoulder and went at the ground with a shovel. Looking around at the rest of all the junk, Brianna found an old hoe, and the two of them dug and dug. The humming blared in her ear until her tool hit something that created a hollow, metallic ding.

But before they could crouch down and dust off the dirt, a blast of wind gusted through, blowing forcefully. Brianna and Jacob raised their hands against the flying dirt, and when they lowered them, they saw a small metal toolbox, rusted thanks to years and years of being buried, sitting before them.

Heart pounding, Brianna bent down and took the padlock of the box in her hand. It was icy cold to the touch. She tugged it, and the rusted metal hinges snapped off.

"How'd you do that?" Jacob asked, his breath coming out in clouds of steam.

"It's Elisa" was all Brianna could say.

Not feeling like she was quite in control, Brianna lifted the lid of the box with a squeaky metallic creak.

A powerful stench hit them. It was so bad, Brianna reared back and tugged her sweater over her nose to get some kind of relief. But that was nothing compared to seeing what lay at the bottom of the box.

16

Elisa's body was no longer a rotting corpse—not after decades. It was a skeleton. A skull with faint wisps of hair and thin ridges of bones under a satin orange dress with a cream ribbon. From the looks of it, because Brianna didn't dare touch it, her whole body was there, all except her foot.

A spider crawled across her dress, and Brianna flinched, her beating heart loud in the sudden silence. The humming was finally gone.

Before Brianna or Jacob could say a word about finding Elisa's skeletal remains, the sound of tires on gravel cut through their stunned silence. Practically jumping out of their skin, they both scrambled to the edge of the wall and peered around the corner.

Emerging from an old SUV was none other than Principal Huckles. Without hesitation, he started toward the back of the building, like he was going to check on something he'd buried years ago.

Jacob and Brianna both glanced back at Elisa's body, realizing at the same time that there was no way they could cover up their discovery. Not before Principal Huckles rounded the corner and found them.

"What do we do?" Jacob whispered. "Do you really think that he—"

"Yes, I think he did," Brianna answered immediately, thinking back to the photo and Uncle Shane's story. What if Principal Huckles had driven the red convertible that night, hit Elisa, buried her at the shop, and then let Uncle Shane have the car and quit his job the next day? He had tried to get as far away from his crime as possible.

How could you drive a car that had killed a little girl? How could you stay at a job where you'd buried her with the rest of the junk?

Thinking fast, Brianna glanced at Jacob's bike, which he'd brought with them. Hers was still in the middle of the parking lot.

"Go back to the festival—get the police and tell them about Elisa."

Jacob was already reaching for his bike. "What about you?"

"While he's distracted, I'll go another way. If we split up, he can't catch us both."

Principal Huckles was already less than ten feet away.

"Go!" Brianna urged.

Jacob jumped on his bike and pedaled fast around the corner of the building, nearly knocking over his surprised principal.

Principal Huckles gave a shout and, as Brianna was hoping he'd do, chased after Jacob. But a bike was too fast for him, and he bent over, wheezing, at the edge of the road. Knowing it was only a matter of time before he went back to check on Elisa's burial place, Brianna darted out from her hiding place and raced for her bike. She grabbed its handles and heaved it up.

"HEY!" Principal Huckles's shout traveled across the parking lot.

Heavy footsteps thudded after her, and Brianna didn't have time to think—she just turned and jumped on the bike, pedaling through the grass and into the nearby woods.

Just as cold shade fell upon her shoulders, she heard an angry shout come from behind. Principal Huckles had found what Brianna and Jacob had dug up—his biggest, deadliest secret.

"I'LL GET YOU, YOU BRAT!"

Even though it was still a chilly October day, Brianna was already sweating. A different kind of fear grabbed hold of her. She wasn't running from a ghost now. She was running from a real flesh-and-blood killer.

Then something even worse happened. Her tire hit a rock or a tree root, and she went sprawling into the grass. With a groan of pain, she picked herself up and just ran as fast as she could. If she kept going in this direction, eventually she should hit the town road again. Maybe then she'd find *someone* who could help her.

Tears of panic and fear blurring her vision and a sob catching in her throat, Brianna ran faster and faster as heavy feet crashed through the woods behind her.

Run. Run. Run.

Although Brianna had a decent head start, Principal Huckles had longer legs, and she could hear him gaining on her.

She dodged and wove around each tree, simply trying to lose him through the thick foliage. Only he was too fast for her.

Branches hit her arms, and thorns and brambles scratched and pulled at her jeans. Just as the panic in her chest threatened to stop her breathing, Brianna burst through the tree line and hit the pavement of a road that she knew very well.

Shadowrun Road.

But how had she made it here? Had the auto shop been closer than what she'd thought? Or was it due to something more...sinister? Shadowrun Road looked different than normal. In the middle of the day, when it should've been bright and sunny, it was the place of her many nightmares.

The whole road was covered in darkness. It was like the shadows of the trees had expanded, enveloping the entire road to make it more like a real tunnel instead of just one made by nature.

It was so dark that Brianna could barely see two steps in front of her. And it was deathly cold. Colder than it had ever been. Colder than the Arctic.

Barely fifteen seconds later, a second pair of heavy footsteps hit the pavement, and Brianna whirled around. In the strange and sudden darkness, she'd forgotten that Principal Huckles had been chasing after her. But now here he was—only a few feet away. Within reach.

"I ... I knew whenever you ... wouldn't stop talking about that stupid ghost ..." Principal Huckles panted as he took another step toward her.

Brianna's lungs were shriveled in the cold, her pulse was pounding in her neck, and her muscles and side screamed at her for sprinting through the woods. She was exhausted.

So when Principal Huckles stepped toward her, cold fury on his face and his hands outstretched as if to grab her, she couldn't even move another inch.

"And then I saw that you'd taken my photo in my office ..." He was just a few feet away from her now—then he lunged for her!

A scream built up in Brianna's chest, when all of a sudden a flock of crows dropped down from the trees and attacked Principal Huckles. He cried out, covering his face from the beating wings and piercing beaks and claws. Then, just as suddenly, the crows flew away, and he lowered his arms, his expression transforming from one of anger to one of absolute terror. His eyes grew wide, and his jaw dropped, bottom lip and hands trembling as he looked on at Brianna.

"N-no, p-please," he stuttered, staring at Brianna in horror. His skin was as pale as if he'd seen a—

Brianna looked over her shoulder.

There was Elisa.

The ghost of Shadowrun Road stood a few feet away. Her dress was streaked in dirt and leaves, her lips were blue, and her eyes were as black as the surrounding forest.

She stepped forward.

STOMP, shhh, shhh.

"Noooo!" Principal Huckles moaned, covering his ears with his hands. "Please, go away!" he begged, his voice howling with the wind that began to shake through the trees.

Brianna moved to the side, allowing Elisa to limp past her—toward her killer.

STOMP, shhh, shhh. STOMP, shhh, shhh.

"Leave me alone!" Principal Huckles cried, raking his hands through his thinning hair. He took a step back as Elisa limped forward.

Overhead, the trees themselves shuddered. Like gigantic dark hands of witches, the branches reached down as if in hopes of trapping the principal within Shadowrun Road—like how Elisa had been trapped there for so, so long.

At the end of the road, two bright yellow headlights blinked into existence. The sound of the powerful engine echoed within the dark tunnel. *VROOOOM*.

While Principal Huckles jerked around to look at the red convertible at the end of the tunnel, gunning its motor toward him, Elisa grabbed Principal Huckles around the middle. Like she wanted to hold him in place.

Meanwhile, the car sped toward all three of them, getting ever closer, its gold headlights shining into the cursed darkness.

Brianna raised her hand against the sheer

brightness and the leaves slapping her cheeks. She screamed over the wind and the roar of Elisa's red monster. "Admit what you did! Tell the truth!"

The car got closer and closer.

VROOM.

VROOM.

VROOM.

The headlights were like two miniature balls of fire speeding toward them—coming from beyond the gates of the afterlife.

"All right! All right!" Principal Huckles screamed. "I killed her! But it was just an accident! An accident!"

The car blew into them like another gust of strong wind—disappearing in a poof of exhaust smoke and shadows.

Principal Huckles dropped to his knees, sobbing, while Elisa stepped back from her hold on him.

Stomp, shh, shh.

As she did so, the overhanging branches retreated, the sky grew lighter, and the winds calmed down to a gentle breeze. A familiar pickup truck turned onto the road, honking its horn repeatedly.

Uncle Shane.

Brianna tore her eyes away from her uncle's truck to see Elisa standing over her sobbing killer with a triumphant smile on her blue lips.

17

As the truck screeched to a stop a few feet away, Brianna felt Elisa's presence leave entirely. The rest of the shadows retreated, and the freezing arctic cold warmed to a nippy October chill.

To Brianna's surprise, both Uncle Shane and Jacob jumped out of the truck. Uncle Shane ran over to her and wrapped her up in a big bear hug. "You scared the tar out of me, Brianna!" he said as he squeezed her tight.

Once he let her go, Brianna glanced from Jacob to her uncle. "What . . . ? How did you know?"

"Jacob found me and told me everything. The police are on their way here—and to the auto shop." Uncle Shane swallowed hard, glaring down at his old friend and coworker, who was still crying and mumbling Elisa's name over and over. "All these years, she deserved better than that, Drew Huckles. Shame on you."

Then he turned to Brianna and knelt beside her. "Thank you for listening to Elisa, kid. When no one else in this town would."

Tears in her eyes, Brianna hugged her uncle back. "I knew it couldn't be you," she muttered into his flannel plaid shirt.

Just then, sirens echoed through the tunnel of trees. As two police cars came zooming down Shadowrun Road, Uncle Shane guided Brianna and Jacob safely inside his truck. "You two wait in here, all right?"

When the police cars stopped next to Uncle Shane, the mayor, along with a few other police officers of Drury Gables, got out and surrounded Principal Huckles. While the adults talked to Elisa's murderer and locked handcuffs around his wrists, Brianna and Jacob watched from Uncle Shane's truck.

"So, do you think Elisa can finally rest in peace?" Jacob asked.

Brianna looked around at the road. Sunlight poured through the leaves, creating those beautiful patterns that Brianna had sketched in what felt like ages ago.

"I hope so."

∾ 🎃 ∾

A good chunk of the rest of the day was spent at the police station, answering whatever questions the sheriff asked. The sheriff muttered something about leaving out the ghost details in his report.

By the time she was finally free to go, it was nearly dusk, but Uncle Shane surprised her by taking both her and Jacob back to the Annual Pumpkin Festival to join in on the fun. They had grilled corn, pumpkin pie, and funnel cake, and played carnival games like the bean bag toss and musical chairs. Later, Jacob's mother and father joined them, and they finished off the evening with a hay ride and the corn maze. Brianna was shocked at how good her uncle was at mazes when he led them through in less than twenty minutes.

It was the most fun Brianna had ever had in Drury Gables, and when night came at last, she was almost sorry that she would have to leave tomorrow.

The next morning, Brianna towed her suitcase down the steps and found Uncle Shane waiting at the bottom of the stairs.

He handed her a slender box wrapped with brown paper and twine. "Gotcha something. Just open it."

Curious, Brianna pulled off the string and ripped open the paper. It was a beautiful new set of sketching pencils. Brianna was speechless. She hadn't even been aware that Uncle Shane had known she liked drawing.

"Wow. Thank you, Uncle Shane."

He stuck his hands in his pockets, and Brianna could've sworn he was blushing. "Don't mention it."

Her throat feeling a little tight with emotion, she followed Uncle Shane out the door as he took her suitcase and put it into the back of the truck. She couldn't believe that after weeks of desperately wanting to leave Drury Gables, she was actually sad to go.

Just as Brianna was about to get into the truck, she heard her name called from around the bend in the trees.

"Brianna! Bree!"

Jacob Dorham swerved onto the driveway of the farmhouse, a flurry of leaves kicked up by the thin tires of his bike. He pedaled hard all the way across the gravel as Brianna dropped her backpack and rushed to meet him halfway.

"Jacob! What are you doing here?" she asked, unable to stop a grin that stretched across her face. They had said their goodbyes yesterday evening when leaving the festival, but she had to admit she was happy to see him one more time before she left.

Still panting, clearly having biked hard all the way here, Jacob jumped off his bike and steadied it with his kickstand. "I've got something for you."

Instantly, Brianna felt guilty. If it was a goodbye present, she hadn't gotten him anything.

But he didn't pull out a wrapped package like Uncle Shane. Instead, he pulled out a photograph from his back pocket and handed it to her. "I had my dad print one for me, too," he explained, his freckled face growing red.

It was a photo that Jacob's dad had taken the day before. The two of them were surrounded by piles of hay and a dozen pumpkins, and they were eating caramel apples. Their fingers were sticky, and they were both smiling and waving.

It was so strange. When Brianna had arrived in Drury Gables, she hadn't had one single memory of the place, and she hadn't cared to remember it at all. But now that she was leaving, she had so many memories she hoped she'd never forget. Even some of the scary ones.

Jacob must've taken Brianna's awe at the photo for dislike, because he hurriedly explained, "I just thought since you had that picture of Elisa, and one of the red convertible, that you needed, you know . . ."

Brianna reached over and gave Jacob a quick hug.

Jacob blinked at her in surprise. "What was that for?"

"The picture. And I really couldn't have helped Elisa without you. So . . . thanks."

Jacob smiled back. "Will you be visiting your uncle again?"

Brianna glanced back at the truck, where her uncle sat patiently waiting with the engine running. "I think I'll definitely come back to Drury Gables."

∽ 🎃 ∼

The ride to the Philadelphia airport was long, and try as she might, Brianna couldn't keep her eyes open. As they passed rolling hills and thick forests vacant of their lovely autumn colors, Brianna slipped off into her first pleasant dream in months . . .

The pumpkin in her arms felt light as a feather. Behind her was a world of shadows and cold, empty darkness, but what lay ahead was a golden magical forest where elves and fairies might live. The red, orange, and yellow leaves from the overhanging branches created a lovely pattern across the light gray asphalt. Beyond the trees was a clear blue sky where the calls of geese leaving for the winter could be heard over the soft whisper of the October breeze. The color of the sky was the same color as her first-place ribbon.

Skipping down the road, she passed a house, but it was not hers. She had just a little bit farther to go. It wouldn't be long now. She rounded the bend in the trees and stepped off Shadowrun Road onto her driveway.

She was home, at long last.

Acknowledgments

When I first thought of Drury Gables, I thought of the sleepy little Pennslyvania town my father grew up in. The place I visited every summer and winter to see my grandparents will forever live within this book. (Although there wasn't a ghost in that town—that I knew of.)

Thank you to my wonderful editor, Orlando Dos Reis, and his endless patience and support while I wrote, revised, and brainstormed how to execute the same scene over and over again. A round of applause to Caroline Flanagan, Jackie Hornberger, Emily Epstein White,

Jessica White, and Lori Lewis. And many thanks to Frances Black, my agent over at Literary Counsel.

Finally, a quick shout-out to the Doylestown Bookshop and the Bucks County Bookfest for being a source of inspiration (and the place where I wrote a large chunk of this book).

About the Author

Lindsey Duga is a middle-grade and young adult writer with a passion for fantasy, science fiction, and basically any genre that takes you away from the real world. She holds a bachelor's degree in mass communication from Louisiana State University. She lives in Baton Rouge, Louisiana.